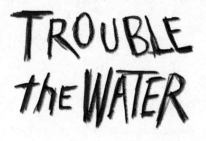

Also by Frances O'Roark Dowell

Anybody Shining
Chicken Boy
Dovey Coe
Falling In
The Second Life of Abigail Walker
Shooting the Moon
Ten Miles Past Normal
Where I'd Like to Be

* * *

The Secret Language of Girls
The Kind of Friends We Used to Be
The Sound of Your Voice, Only Really Far Away

* * *

Phineas L. MacGuire . . . Blasts Off!
Phineas L. MacGuire . . . Erupts!
Phineas L. MacGuire . . . Gets Slimed!
Phineas L. MacGuire . . . Gets Cooking!

TROUBLE the WATER

FRANCES O'ROARK DOWELL

A Caitlyn Dlouhy Book

A Atheneum Books for Young Readers
New York   London   Toronto   Sydney   New Delhi

atheneum

ATHENEUM BOOKS FOR YOUNG READERS
An imprint of Simon & Schuster Children's Publishing Division
1230 Avenue of the Americas, New York, New York 10020

ATHENEUM BOOKS FOR YOUNG READERS is a registered trademark of Simon & Schuster, Inc.
Atheneum logo is a trademark of Simon & Schuster, Inc.
For information about special discounts for bulk purchases, please contact Simon & Schuster Special Sales at 1-866-506-1949 or business@simonandschuster.com.
The Simon & Schuster Speakers Bureau can bring authors to your live event. For more information or to book an event, contact the Simon & Schuster Speakers Bureau at 1-866-248-3049 or visit our website at www.simonspeakers.com.
Book design by Sonia Chaghatzbanian
The text for this book is set in Palatino.
Manufactured in the United States of America
0716 FFG

10 9 8 7 6 5 4 3
Library of Congress Cataloging-in-Publication Data
Dowell, Frances O'Roark.
Trouble the water / Frances O'Roark Dowell.
pages cm
ISBN 978-1-4814-2463-9 (hardcover)
ISBN 978-1-4814-2465-3 (eBook)
[1. Race relations—Fiction.
2. Segregation—Fiction. 3. African Americans—Fiction.
4. Dogs—Fiction. 5. Family life—Kentucky—Fiction.
6. Underground Railroad—Fiction. 7. Kentucky—History—20th century—Fiction.] I. Title.
PZ7.D75455Tro 2017   [Fic]—dc23   2014045331

For my very favorite nephew,
Devin Jonikas O'Roark

Acknowledgments

First and foremost, I'd like to thank Caitlyn Dlouhy, as usual, as always, with love. What a thrill to have your name on the cover of this book! Thanks to Jessica Sit, who is so, so talented and so very kind, and thanks to Justin Chanda, whom I feel lucky to know and have on my side. Thanks to Clare McGlade, copyeditor extraordinaire, and to Sonia Chaghatzbanian for yet another beautifully designed book. I'm grateful for the many fine resources that informed the writing of *Trouble the Water*, including *The Hidden Wound* by Wendell Berry, *Front Line of Freedom: African Americans and the Forging of the Underground Railroad in the Ohio Valley* by Keith Griffler, and *Community Memories: A Glimpse of African American Life in Frankfort, Kentucky* edited by Winona L. Fletcher.

Finally, thanks to my family—Clifton, Jack, and Will; and thanks to my boon companion, Travis, because there's nothing better in this world than a dog.

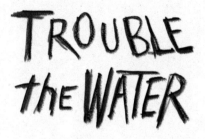

1

The Old Dog

The dog was old and close to dying. He woke slowly now that he was back, the sun warming the ache out of his bones. He had a flickering thought that he'd like to fall asleep and never wake, but he couldn't die until he knew the boy was safe. So every morning he pushed himself up and sniffed the air for the boy's scent, and when he didn't find any trace of it, he started for the river.

Most nights he slept on the woman's porch, so that he could smell the river, hear the boy's calls if they came. His first night back, he'd gone

1

to his old house, but when he'd barked, no one had opened the door or called out, "Hey, pup, ready for dinner?" If the boy had been there, he would have answered.

He knew that the woman would give him scraps from the table in a bowl by the door when she saw him, and he knew that if he stayed too long, she'd try to claim him. She'd snapped a collar on him when he showed up the first time, but he'd complained so loudly that she'd finally taken it off. The old dog, like most dogs, couldn't parse out the particulars of human speech, but he could make sense of what people were telling or asking him from the pitch of their voices, the firmness or wobble of their words, so he'd known the woman wanted him to stay when she'd said, "You'd like it here, I swear you would," before she put the collar back on a peg just inside the door-way.

The woman lived in the house by herself. No other human smells mixed with hers, no onion stink of a man home from the fields, no sweet scent of a child fresh out of his bath, traces of soap still in his hair, an untouched patch of dirt behind his left ear. The old dog had lived close to humans when he was young, close to the boy, and could sniff one on the air. They each had a particular smell, and there was only one human smell around the woman's house. It was a nice smell, a mix of river water and new grass and something sweet. The first small flowers of May. He didn't have words for any of these things, but he knew them.

"Well, hey there, pup," the woman greeted him now as she emerged from the doorway with a basket in her hand. "I see you stayed for breakfast. Look at you, so slow to get up. Bet you got the arthritis in your bones, old thing like you."

He followed her around the corner of the house and through the garden gate. "Got to get your vegetables picked first thing of a morning," the woman informed him as she set to work. "Bugs'll eat you alive if you come out here at night, skeeters and no-see-ums, they'll bite you all to pieces. Sun'll burn you up, you come out at noon. No, first thing of a morning,

3

that's the best time. That's when you get things at their freshest."

As she talked, she pulled tomatoes and squash and cucumbers off their vines and put them in her basket. The old dog sniffed the vegetables without much interest. Sometimes the woman scrambled him a pan of eggs, and cooked a few slices of bacon, and at the last minute threw in leftovers from dinner the night before. He knew all he had to do was follow along as she did her morning chores and chatted to him. The old dog liked the woman. He didn't mind waiting.

Breakfast this morning turned out to be fried liver mush and cold roasted potatoes. He gulped down the liver in two swallows and sniffed the air for more. "Sorry, pup, you got the last of it," the woman told him. "Come back tonight, I might have some chicken for you. I'll take out the bones first, lessen you choke."

The old dog recognized the sound in her voice as something he'd been feeling so long now it was like a natural-born part of him. It was the sound of something—someone—missing.

4

On his long journey home, his nose in the air, hunting for the boy's scent, he'd let out a howl now and again, and you could hear that sound in his voice too.

After breakfast he left the woman's house for the woods and the river, and was almost at the water when he heard a younger dog barking. How far away? Far enough that he couldn't be sure what—or who—the younger dog was growling at. Maybe the old dog, but probably not. He understood other dogs even better than he understood humans. Still, he took cover.

When he sensed the danger was past, he slowly took to his feet again. Should he go back to the woman's house, rest under the cool shade of her front porch? When the sun got low enough in the sky, she'd come out to keep him company, and he liked that, liked her voice as it went up and down and drifted through his dreams.

He was about to turn around when a feeling seized him, shot through his chest and around his ears like a winter wind. *Follow the dog*, the feeling told him. Sniffing the air, he understood. It wasn't just a dog in the woods; the wind carried the scent of a boy. And though he knew it wasn't *his* boy, maybe this boy could lead him to his boy.

The old dog was dying. He knew he was dying. He knew he didn't have much time. He turned and headed deep into the woods.

2

Callie, at Least
a Little Bit Free

allie wasn't supposed to leave the yard until she finished weeding, but when that yellow dog trotted by, she just had to follow him. She'd seen the dog three days in a row now, after never having seen him even once in her life, and she was feeling curious about him. She knew all the dogs in the Bottom, and this dog wasn't one of them. He was an old dog, by the looks of him, the way the fur around his eyes was white and his gait had a little bit of a hitch in it. But there was no doubt about it—old or not, the dog was on the move.

Callie tugged at a clump of crabgrass and wondered why a dog would just appear out of thin air and start patrolling her neighborhood, looking this way and that, like he was some kind of detective dog, out solving some kind of dog crime. Callie'd asked everybody she knew about him, but no one had the slightest idea who he was or who his people might be. He was too old to be somebody's new dog, that was for sure. When people got themselves a dog, they wanted a young pup. Wanted a dog with a little get-along in his step.

Callie decided today was the day she was going to follow the dog and find out his story. Fact was, she was bored to death and needed to be on the move herself. She was supposed to go inside and eat lunch, an old wopsided peanut butter sandwich most likely, because Regina was in charge of lunch, and Regina couldn't put two slices of bread together straightaways for the life of her. If Carl Jr. were home, he'd do a better job, maybe stick a slice of bacon in the sandwich to give it some salt and crunch, but he'd walked over to McKinley's Drug to eyeball some comic books. Mama'd kill him if she knew. "White folks don't like you doing nothing in their stores but for coming in, putting your money down, and going out," Mama told them every time she sent one of them to the drugstore or to the A&P grocery. Mama was always worrying about what white folks would do or say or think.

But Carl Jr. wasn't worried about nothing. You thought you heard a ghost up in your room, he was the person you needed to call. He'd come stomping in, yell, "You get yourself out of here, Mr. Ghost! I don't even believe in you, but if I did, I'd smash you all to pieces." That would make Callie laugh so hard, she'd forget about being scared of moaning, groaning ghosts and one-eyed, gape-mouthed monsters who liked to finish up their day by snacking on sweet-tasting children such as herself.

Now Callie stood up and looked over the flower bed she was supposed to get done weeding before Mama got home from her cleaning job at Mrs. Whitson's. That flower bed was Mama's pride and joy, but Callie was sick to death of it. Oh, she loved working down on her knees after the last frost and helping Mama drop in the tee-tiny seeds—this one a quarter inch under the dirt, this one barely under the dirt at all—Callie was careful about doing it just right. She loved watching the first leaves push themselves up through the dirt to catch sight of the sun. Most of all she loved watching the flowers start to bloom, all the pretty colors waving at you from in front of the porch.

What Callie didn't love was the weeds—the burdock, the bindweed, the prickly thistles, the dandelions—in fact, she hated weeds worse than anything else she could think of. So how come she got elected head weed picker of the household? She understood why Daddy couldn't do it, working from dawn till dusk at the paper mill, and she understood why Mama might not want to get down on her knees after a long day spent scrubbing folks' floors. But Carl Jr. and Regina were free as the wind on a summer morning, so why didn't they have to come out and help her?

Carl Jr. would shake his head sadly when

Callie asked him. "'Cause we don't love the flowers the way you do, Little Sis. We don't *understand* them the way you do. We'd be pulling up daffodils instead of dandelions."

"Mama don't grow daffodils," Callie would argue. "'Sides, daffodils come up in the spring. They die back in the summertime heat."

"See, Little Sis, that's what I'm telling you," Carl Jr. would insist. "You know all them important floral facts. Me and Regina, we're dopes when it comes to flowers."

"When Mama's gone, I'm in charge of the house," Regina insisted if Callie said she should come outside and help. "The *inside* of the house. I ain't got time for weeding."

That always made Callie grumble. As far as she could tell, all Regina did was wipe the crumbs off the counter ten minutes before Mama was supposed to get home in the afternoon. Otherwise, Regina, who was only three years older, if anybody was counting, lay around on the couch in the front room reading books from the stack she brought home from the library each week.

So when the old yellow dog walked past Callie on the sidewalk right before lunchtime, she took it as a sign. She'd been waiting for something interesting to happen all summer. That's what she dreamed about locked up in school, her legs itching inside the wool tights Mama made her wear from the first of November till the last day of March. Every scratch old Miss Pettigrew made on the chalkboard sent an electric buzz up Callie's spine and was even more torturous to her than her itchy tights. The only relief she got was imagining the sort of adventures she'd have once she was free.

Well, she was free now, or at least halfway, sort of, a little bit free. Free from being stuck in that old fifth grade, anyway. She plucked a handful of clover from over by the delphiniums and wiped the dirt from her hands. She'd finish up her weeding later in the day, when the shade had made its way to the front yard. Crashing into the house and beelining it for the kitchen, she yelled, "Regina, you got my sandwich ready yet?"

"It's on the counter," her sister called from

12

the front room. "Not that I'm your servant, Little Miss Bossy. A 'please' and 'thank you' might be nice."

"Please and thank you," Callie muttered, wrapping the pathetic excuse for a sandwich she found on the counter—peanut butter and grape jelly, with a wilted lettuce leaf hanging from the sides of the store-bought bread—in a kitchen towel. "I'm taking my sandwich on the road like a hobo," she called more loudly on her way back to the front door. "I'll be home before Mama gets back."

"You best not be going to Cecily's," Regina hollered after her. "You don't do nothing but get in trouble over at that girl's house. It's like the two of you lose all sense when you get together."

The screen door slammed behind Callie in a satisfying way. She'd let that be the answer to Regina's harping. Regina was just jealous that Callie had a best friend. Regina's best friend, Ruthie Owens, had moved up to Ohio at the end of the school year with her family because her daddy had heard there were good jobs to be had up around Youngstown and he aimed to get himself one, get out of the stink of the paper mill, he said.

Callie thought the idea of moving somewhere else was exciting, and had tried to convince Mama and Daddy that they ought to move up to Youngstown, Ohio, too.

"Who would take care of Mama Lou and Pap if we moved to Ohio?" Mama had asked. "You want to leave those old folks to fend for themselves?"

"They could go with us," Callie had insisted, but she knew her grandparents wouldn't ever set foot outside of Celeste, Kentucky. Mama Lou might be near a hundred (or maybe sixty, it was all the same to Callie), but she was the pillar and post of the Rock of Ages Seventh-Day Adventist Church over on Lexington Street, and she probably would be till the day she died. You couldn't pry Mama Lou away from that church with a crowbar. Why, the walls might fall down without her.

"We're stuck like a truck bogged down in the muck," Callie complained to the air, running a stick across Mrs. Strummer's picket fence to hear the satisfying click of it. She didn't *really* feel all that stuck; at least when she wasn't in school, she didn't. Celeste, Kentucky, wasn't the worst place in the world. Didn't have volcanoes here, no pit vipers hissing at you from folks' yards, no monsters, least none that came out during daylight hours. Even the white folks weren't that bad, for white folks. Daddy said if you went down to some place like Mississippi or Alabama, you'd meet some real mean white people who'd hang you from a tree soon as look at you. Mama always hushed him when he said that, but Daddy said that, no, Regina, Carl Jr., and Callie needed to know the truth about the world, and truth was, even at the late date of 1953, there were some folks who'd kill you 'cause you were a different color or religion, or even just because you had an original opinion.

White folks in Celeste mostly seemed cranky and full of themselves to Callie, though sometimes they could be downright rude. You could be waiting your turn in the checkout line at the grocery, polite as could be, and if a white lady came in, she'd cut straight in front of you, even if you were with a grown-up. Colored folks had to sit in the balcony at the movies, though the only reason Callie minded was because it was a rule. As far as she was concerned, the balcony was the place to be, way up high, with a good view of everything. White folks could have the orchestra seats, for all she cared, sitting down there with their eyes all squinched up from being too close to the screen.

The sidewalk's heat seeped up through the soles of Callie's sneakers. Man alive, it was hot. She wondered if it was even worth it to follow the old yellow dog, get all sweaty, come home dirty with leaves stuck in her hair. She could go to Cecily's instead, except she and Cecily were feuding, and Cecily's mama, Mrs. Perkins, wouldn't even let Callie into the house when she and Cecily were in a fighting mood. "I ain't gonna have my whole day spoiled by you two girls yelping and yapping about who started it and who did what to who. You cool your heads a couple days, you'll figure out a way to work things out."

Now Callie tried to remember what the feud was about. What had gotten her and Cecily so mad at each other? She turned south on Marigold Lane, her brain trying to latch on to the reason she'd stomped out of the Perkinses' house yesterday morning. What did she and Cecily usually fight about? Who was the best, mostly. In some categories they didn't have no cause to argue. Cecily was best at composition writing and memorizing history facts. Callie was best at mathematics and running fast. No need to argue there. So what was it?

Veering off the sidewalk onto a dirt path, still heading south, Callie suddenly remembered. They'd been feuding over whose mama had the prettiest dresses. Now, while Callie didn't care so much about the clothes she herself wore (they were always getting mucked up as soon as she stepped out of the house— Mama said Callie was a dirt magnet, attracting every speck of dirt and dust and grime from five miles around), she did have a soft spot for nice clothes on other people, and everybody knew for a fact that her mama sewed some of

17

the prettiest dresses ever seen in Celeste, Kentucky. Fancy, colorful dresses with swirling skirts and cute collars. Callie always felt proud walking next to Mama down the sidewalk of a Sunday on their way to church. She had the prettiest mama wearing the prettiest dress, and everybody knew it.

Now, she wouldn't say that Mrs. Bernice Perkins did not have style. Oh, that Mrs. Perkins could wear herself a hat, and Callie was the first person to admit it. Mrs. Perkins also had a way with a handbag. But dresses as pretty as Mama's? Uh-uh. Don't even think it.

The dirt path pushed its way into the woods behind Widow Kendall's house, and Callie brushed back some branches scratching at her face. She hoped that old Mrs. Kendall wasn't out back tending to her garden. "Ornery" was the word for that woman. She'd start yelling about private property and trespassing, even though everybody knew didn't nobody own the woods. Woods were free places that couldn't be bought up. Carl Jr. said that wasn't necessarily so, but Callie thought it should be

18

the rule, so in her mind it *was* a rule. Woods = free place, no bosses.

She kept on walking, but now she was keeping an eye out for the old yellow dog. She couldn't know for sure he'd gone down to the river, but it made sense he would on a day as hot as this, and the path through the woods was the way most folks got down to the water. She and Daddy walked this way to go fishing, but Mrs. Kendall never hollered at Daddy. She'd wave a hand and maybe start talking about her tomatoes, how the bonemeal she'd been feeding them was doing the trick. Daddy always made a little conversation with Mrs. Kendall, hushing Callie if she hissed, *C'mon, Daddy, let's go.*

When she heard the barking, it seemed to come from a long ways off, and it didn't sound like the yellow dog's, an old dog's bark, sad sounding and weary. This bark she was hearing now was full of meaning. Vigorous. Maybe some other dog had seen the old yellow dog and was calling to it. Daddy said most of the time when you heard dogs bark, even though it might sound gruff and warning-like, mostly it was dogs asking questions of one another: *Who are you? Where you from? Do I got some reason to be concerned about you?*

Callie thought this particular bark might be a *Who are you?* bark, and she decided to follow it, thinking it might get her to the old yellow dog and closer to finding out what he was up to. She bet that old dog was looking for somebody. In fact, Callie could feel it in her bones. Callie, well, she was looking for the story, and since nobody else knew what it was, she'd have to track it down herself.

3

Jim, the Almost-Visible Boy

Hardly a day passed that Jim Trebble didn't think about how a big, juicy hamburger from Burger World would taste, tucked into a sesame seed bun with a slice of tomato and a crisp piece of lettuce. Fred used to could down three of 'em at one sitting, plus an order of onion rings and a thick chocolate milk shake. Jim had worked up to two burgers and a plateful of french fries, but anything more made him feel like his belly might bust wide open.

"You ain't a man till you can eat three," Fred had teased him, and three Burger World

21

hamburgers had been Jim's goal ever since, if only he could remember where Burger World was. Out on Route 16 somewhere, but he couldn't think of the exact spot, and anyway, that was too far for him to go. He could make it into town, and once he'd even gotten out to Uncle Owen's farm, but past that, the edges of the world seemed to dissolve into a foggy bog, and Jim was afraid to go any farther.

When he wasn't thinking about hamburgers, he was thinking about meat loaf and mashed potatoes, pumpkin pie, turkey with gravy and dressing at Thanksgiving, rare roast beef on Christmas Eve. He liked to dream about chocolate cake, baked potatoes, sweet potato casserole, and corn on the cob fresh from the garden. He even pondered crisp cucumbers from time to time, even though he'd never liked cucumbers all that much. But you'll get to missing anything if you haven't had a bite of it in longer than you can recall.

Jim tried to eat. Tried as hard as he could. Problem was, everything slipped through his fingers before it got to his mouth. Just this morning he'd gone to pick a honeysuckle blossom to get a little taste of nectar, but when he'd reached to pinch the flower off the vine, it was like his fingers were made of air. He could see them, so he was pretty sure they were there, but for some reason nothing else knew it. He'd cup his hands to get a sip of water from the creek, and the water would ignore him, slipping past his fingers like they didn't exist.

So Jim wasn't sure if they did or not.

The sun was getting high in the sky when Jim heard the dog bark, which meant that boy Wendell was out and about tramping through the woods. Jim stepped through the door and checked for his shadow, the same way he'd done every day since the beginning of the summer, when he'd woken up to find himself in the cabin, wondering what he was doing there. There'd been a dog then, too, barking in the distance, and it had sounded so much like his dog, Buddy, that Jim had rolled over and mumbled, *Hush, boy, I'm still sleeping*. But when he'd opened his eyes, he hadn't been in his room. It had been the strangest thing in the world.

Now, outside, he looked at the ground. His shadow still wasn't there. It confounded him, not having a shadow anymore. If he were invisible, he could understand it. But he knew in broad daylight folks could see him, at least a little, tiny bit. He'd found his way to Granny's house a few weeks ago, to see what she was fixing for lunch. She'd looked straight at him and backed into the table, rattling the ice in the tea pitcher.

"That you, Jim?" she'd asked in a trembling voice. "I don't believe it could be, now could it?"

It's me, Jim insisted, but Granny didn't appear to hear.

"Lord, son, we've been missing you a long time," Granny went on, and Jim waited to hear more, waited for Granny to tell him where everyone else had gone to and explain why he could find her house, just couldn't seem to find his own. But she started crying instead. Jim tried to pat her on the shoulder in a comforting way, but when he touched her, she shivered, and he thought he'd best leave her alone. On his way out he glanced in the mirror in the

24

front hallway, and there he was—Jim Trebble, age twelve, a little bit see-through, a little bit shiny around the edges, but it was definitely him.

Now when he went out during daylight, he stayed to the shadows and the shady parts. No point scaring folks to death.

He hadn't seen Wendell in a week or so. Wendell almost always brought his dog, a redbone hound named King, and he talked that dog's ear off, told him baseball scores and his plans for building a fort in his backyard, if only his dad could get some time off from the mill. Jim could picture that fort, high up in a tree, with good, strong walls to keep the enemy out. He knew just how to build a fort like that, and it drove him crazy that he couldn't give Wendell some help, that he couldn't even get Wendell to see that he was there.

He caught up with Wendell near the creek. Wendell's nose was peeling from a sunburn, and Jim remembered how he always got sunburned in the summer. But now his skin was pale, hardly even a color. King looked over when Jim got close, the way he always did, and Jim wondered if the dog could see him even though he was standing in the shade of an oak tree. Folks said dogs had all sorts of abilities humans didn't know about, and Jim believed it. In his opinion, most people weren't half as smart as a dog. His own dog, Buddy, was a superior creature to himself in almost every way, except that he couldn't talk, and even there Jim thought Buddy was just holding back, not wanting to show off.

"Come here, boy," Jim called to King, and to his surprise the dog growled, a deep-throated growl that made Jim step even farther back into the shadows, and then let out a deep bay that lifted into a chorus of short, high-pitched barks.

"What is it, boy?" Wendell asked, looking around. A cloud passed over the sun. "Come on, King. Let's head for the river." King gave out one more low growl, a warning to whatever— or whoever—was out there, and then trotted over to Wendell's side. They set out walking again.

Jim didn't follow. He hunkered in the shadows, trembling a little. He'd known King for a while now, and the dog had never growled at him before. It felt to Jim like the dog had turned against him somehow. That confused him and made him feel lonesome. He only had a few friends now, and he'd counted King among them.

The birds in the trees overhead chattered feverishly among themselves. Jim turned to head back to the cabin, not bothering to stay out of the sun's way. He hated it when Wendell went to the river. It gave Jim a sick feeling to even get near the water, which was funny, since he could remember fishing down there with Daddy and Fred and Uncle Owen, and a long time ago he used to go swimming at the bend with his friends. Not with Wendell, though. Jim hadn't met Wendell until—well, Jim wasn't so good with time anymore. He couldn't exactly remember when he'd met Wendell.

The sun beat against Jim's back. He could feel the sense of it, if not the heat. He held up his hand and waved it around, but still no shadow. He kept waving and waving, though, and then, just for a second, he thought he saw a hint of a dark patch against the dirt.

Well, what do you know about that? he thought. He looked around to see if there were any witnesses to this amazing event.

But he was all by himself except for the birds, who went on chirping and twittering as if nothing had happened and nobody at all was there.

4

To Think of Yourself as a River

Even if Callie hadn't taken the path five hundred times, she'd have known she was getting close to the river just by the smell of it. Something wild and a little bit dangerous lifted into the air as you got close to the water. Something that said, *Watch out.*

Didn't scare Callie a bit, of course. She wasn't the kind of girl who was gonna get pulled under by some old river. The way she saw things, she and the river had a lot in common. They both could be calm and relaxed, but you never knew when a storm might stir them up, and when that happened, watch out. "Callie, you better mind your temper, girl," Mama had said on many occasions, and you could say the same thing to a river, now couldn't you? Things could start to boil over in the water, same way they could in Callie's mind, and when that happened, you better scoot up the banks and head for home.

It was satisfying to think of yourself as a river, Callie decided as she made her way down toward the bank. Powerful and mighty at one bend, meek and mild at the next. Well, maybe not meek. Callie had always had problems with that part of the Bible, where Jesus tells everybody, "The meek shall inherit the earth." She'd had to keep herself from shaking her head *uh-uh* right in the middle of church when Pastor Edwards got to that part. Meek folks never got nothing. Weren't no gingersnaps left for the meek children when Mrs. Hudson passed out snacks after the Sunday-school lesson, especially not if Callie Robinson was in their class. Callie was *always* number one in the gingersnap line. Nothing meek about her.

At first Callie didn't see anybody else around, and she didn't see that old dog, either. But when she looked farther down the riverbank, she saw a boy with a red hound standing next to him. The boy was throwing rocks into the water, and the dog was barking at the splashes the rocks made when they hit the water.

Callie stood still as Sunday morning. It wasn't like she'd never seen a white boy down here before, but usually she was with somebody, Daddy or Carl Jr. It felt different being by herself. The boy might think like he could say something to her, something mean and low-down, something that would make Callie feel like she had to defend herself. "White folks give you trouble, you just walk away," Mama always instructed her children, but that didn't sit right with Callie. Someone gave you grief, you had to give them grief right back.

The boy glanced over at Callie, but he didn't say anything, just kept chucking rocks. Callie scooped up a flat stone and skipped it across the water. She'd just ignore that boy, and he'd most likely ignore her, and then one or the other of them would go on their way, no harm done. Maybe the yellow dog would show up, and Callie would follow him and discover his secrets. Maybe she'd write his story up for the *Weekly Advance*, the colored folks' newspaper that came out every Friday. Mr. Renfrow, the editor, liked a good detective-type story. Back in March, Callie had written an article about somebody thieving up and down Church Street, taking small items off of folks' front porches—cigarette lighters, nickels and dimes, keys, and such—and even stealing Mrs. Pinkney's wedding ring right off her kitchen windowsill.

Callie had spent two weeks investigating after school, hiding behind bushes and peeking around corners. The day she saw a bird flying off from Miss Sally Henson's porch with a pink eraser in its mouth, she knew she'd found the culprit. And didn't Mr. Renfrow just eat that story up? Printed it on the front page.

Callie glanced at the boy again. What if the yellow dog had already passed by here and the boy had seen him? Callie could be wasting her time standing where she was. Maybe she should be moving down the riverbank. But how would she know? She ought to ask that boy if he'd seen anything. The boy wasn't going to do nothing to her. He was just an old white boy with his dog. He was probably all right, even if he was white. Daddy said most of the white men he worked with at the paper mill were just fine, didn't give anybody no trouble at all. Maybe this boy's daddy was one of them. Maybe this boy's daddy was the sort of man who told his children, "You be nice to everybody, white or colored."

Besides, you ain't scared of no white boy, she reminded herself. So she yelled across to the boy, "You seen an old yellow dog around here?"

The boy didn't say anything right away, just looked over at her like he was trying to figure out who she was. Finally he yelled back, "He yours?"

"Nah, but I been following him," Callie called. "Trying to figure some things out about him."

33

The boy moved closer to the river's edge, his dog following at his heels. "He won't stay with you. Friend of mine who lives downriver from here tried to tie him up in his backyard the other day. Wanted to make a pet out of him. But the dog howled so hard Will had to let him go."

"Don't want him to stay." Callie took a few steps toward the boy. "My mama won't let us keep a dog for a pet. Cat neither. She don't like fur on her furniture."

"We got three dogs," the boy reported, sounding proud about it. "But we keep 'em outside. Ain't civilized to keep a dog inside."

"I think an inside dog sounds nice. Keep you warm in the wintertime, if he sleeps on the end of your bed."

The boy seemed to consider this. Then he shoved his hands into his pockets and looked up the riverbank. "Anyway, that dog's already been here. What're you looking for him for?"

"Just looking, is all."

The boy nodded. "Well, good luck, then." He whistled to his dog, and the two of them headed up the riverbank into the woods.

Callie watched the boy go, and then sat down on a piece of driftwood. She felt her excitement about chasing after the dog slipping out of her. For all she knew, he was halfway to Covington by now. She scratched at a mosquito bite above her left ankle. *You want to write that article, don't you?* she argued with herself, trying to work up her energy again. She remembered how Daddy had cut her bird article out of the newspaper and carried it in his shirt pocket for a week. Just think how proud he'd be if she had another one in the paper for everybody in the neighborhood to read. He might take it to the mill with him, pass it around.

She stood up and stretched, trying to relight the spark of interest that had gotten her all the way down here at the hottest part of the day, but it was no use. She'd lost her fervor. Callie sighed. She hated when an idea that had held her in its grips suddenly let go. Now she'd have to trudge home, where there wasn't one good thing to do, and nothing much to eat until suppertime. Since she and Cecily weren't speaking to each other, she wouldn't have no one to play with either. But she knew once the excitement of an idea cooled, wasn't nothing she could do to heat it back up. She took off her shoes and walked to the water so she could dip her toes in before heading back on the path toward home.

"Hey, girl!"

Callie turned, and there was the boy and his red hound standing ten yards behind her, where the woods met the riverbank. Fear tugged at Callie's gut. Had he come back to get her? To beat her up and cuss her out?

The boy waved toward the woods. "I just saw him, that dog—up there in the woods, about two hundred yards from here. Come on—I'll show you."

Callie didn't answer. It could be a trick. He might be planning to whup her with a big stick. White boys could get into some evil mischief; she'd heard stories.

"Come on!" the boy insisted. "He's gonna get away if you don't get going."

Callie slowly moved out of the water and picked up her shoes. "You sure it's the old yellow dog?"

"Of course I'm sure. I wouldn't have come back if I wasn't."

Callie slipped her shoes back on. She looked at the boy. How old was he—eleven? Twelve? Hard to tell, but he was pretty scrawny, and Callie thought she could probably take him if he tried to mess with her.

"All right, I'm comin'," she said. "But that dog better be there."

The boy looked at her. "I said he was. Why wouldn't he be?"

"Don't know. Just better be."

The boy mumbled something under his breath, then turned and disappeared back into the woods. Callie followed him. Maybe she was making a mistake, hard to tell. She guessed she was about to find out.

5

Wendell Crow Goes to Town

The day had started out with his dad remembering an old cabin in the woods he and his brothers used to play in when they were boys. "I woke up dreaming about it," he'd said, taking a sip of coffee from his mug that only he could ever drink from, the one with a University of Kentucky blue wildcat growling on it. "Bet it's still there, too. Falling down, most likely. We never could figure out what it was doing there. Hunter might have built it, or somebody who'd cleared the land to settle on it."

Well, of course Wendell immediately wanted to go out looking for that old cabin in the woods, even though his dad couldn't remember exactly where it was, maybe in the woods behind the Jerichos' farm, maybe even closer than that. Wendell thought he'd get George to go with him to find it, and together they could turn it into a place for playing cards and holding secret club meetings and hiding out from their mothers. They'd been needing a place like that for years.

So after he'd finished up his chores, he swung his bike out onto the road and pedaled the two and a half miles to the Franklins', thinking how he wished his family would move into town so that he and George could just stroll in a leisurely-like way to each other's houses, the way boys did in the movies he and his friends sometimes went to see on Saturday mornings. Whole gangs of boys would gather on a street corner at the sound of some kid's whistle. Wendell could whistle all he wanted, but where his house was, out on a county road, only the dogs would come running.

"I bet your dad's making that cabin up," George told Wendell over his bowl of cereal. Summer mornings started late at George's house, all the children still in bed as late as nine, so that Mrs. Franklin could get her housework done in peace.

"He might could be," Wendell admitted, having had that same thought himself riding over. "But he sounded pretty serious about it. I think he was too sleepy to make anything up."

George wiped a dribble of milk from his chin. "I'll go out looking with you tomorrow. Mama's taking us to the swimming pool this morning. You could come."

Wendell weighed this out in his mind. The town swimming pool was new and something of a wonder. For ten cents you could spend all day splashing around, racing up and down the lanes, or wait in line to jump off the high dive, your knees nearly buckling underneath you as you walked the narrow plank out over the water. The joy of it was cut into by all the nervous mothers, George's mother being the worst. The mothers of Celeste, Kentucky, weren't used to swimming pools and were constantly on the lookout in case the water decided to swallow their children up like Jonah's whale.

"I guess not," Wendell said after a minute of thinking on it. "Your mother and everything."

George nodded. He and Wendell had been friends a long time and didn't take offense over much, least of all their mothers.

Wendell decided to ride downtown before going back home. He had a dime in his pocket just waiting to be spent (even though his mother insisted he didn't have to spend every red cent he had—that was her expression, "every red cent," like money came in all the different colors of the rainbow—he could save some of his money, maybe send it to the poor people in Africa, at which point Wendell always started edging out of the room, because when his mother started talking about poor people in Africa, she had a hard time stopping). He thought about comic books and he thought about candy, but he let the thought about candy go, since it was only ten o'clock and already it had to be about ninety degrees.

In this heat a Hershey's bar wouldn't last the bike ride home. It'd be a puddle of chocolate in his pocket, a waste of a nickel.

So probably a comic book, which meant a trip to McKinley's Drug. He pedaled the two blocks over and leaned his bike against the store's brick wall. When he pushed open the door, the smell of ammonia practically clobbered him. Looking around, he didn't see anybody he knew, so he waved at Prissie McKinley, who was over at the ice-cream counter, wiping off the glass cases with Windex and a rag. Prissie was his cousin Mary Anne's best friend, and once, two years ago, she'd given Wendell a free chocolate soda. She hadn't ever done it again since, but Wendell stayed hopeful and was always cordial to her if no one was around to witness it.

There was a colored boy standing in front of the comic-book rack, reading the latest *Spider-Man*, which Wendell had read the week before, standing in that very spot. Wendell had a fifty-fifty arrangement with McKinley's Drug—he bought 50 percent of the new comics on the rack and read the other 50 percent in the store while Mr. McKinley wasn't looking. He was pretty sure Mr. McKinley wasn't aware of this arrangement, but it had a certain logic to Wendell, and he was happy with it.

The colored boy nodded at Wendell, not bothering to unpeel his eyes from the comic book, and Wendell gave a slight nod back. There was a common vocabulary of nods and shrugs among the comic-book readers of McKinley's Drug, who liked to keep things quiet, so as not to draw attention to themselves. It made Wendell a little nervous to stand next to the boy because you never knew who might make a fuss about a colored kid loitering in the store and not moving on about his business. If someone complained, then Wendell would have to move on too, or worse, Mr. McKinley might decide to make a rule about boys standing in front of the comic-book rack for more than a minute, and then Wendell's fifty-fifty arrangement would be done for.

He'd read most all of the comics in front of him, the *Superman* and *The Spirit* and *Captain*

America. There was a new *Wonder Woman,* but Wendell had mixed feelings about *Wonder Woman,* having mixed feelings about females in general, even his mother, who he liked pretty well but thought was too bossy. Besides, he'd never pick up *Wonder Woman* standing next to another boy, even a colored boy. He found a *Batman* he hadn't read and took it up to the counter. Prissie came over and smiled at him but didn't offer any ice cream.

"You going swimming today?" she asked as she rang up the comic book. "I bet there'll be a hundred kids over there." She leaned over the counter toward him and whispered, "You know all those little kids pee in there. I wouldn't swim in that water if you paid me."

Wendell didn't know what to say to that, so he didn't say anything, just took his comic book and gave Prissie a wave good-bye.

Back outside, the hot air pressing hard against him, Wendell abandoned the idea of biking around town. Maybe he'd just go home and read his comic book, or work on making some new bass lures. Last week he'd bought three blocks of balsa wood at the hardware store, but so far all he'd done was trace minnow patterns on them with pencil. Now he could imagine the feel of sitting at the workbench in the corner of the garage, the one little lamp turned on, the damp cool coming up from the cement floor as he whittled the lures with his pocketknife and thought about what colors to paint them.

Wendell headed south out of town and in ten minutes was back home, sweat rolling off his forehead and falling into his eyes. The house was empty when he went inside, so Wendell was free to rummage through the cupboards and refrigerator without anyone commenting on what he was taking or how much. Maybe before he worked on his lures, he could make himself some lunch, take it down to the river. He'd found a good rock a little ways down from the bend, one with a worn, flat place just right for sitting. When he was done eating, he could go to the creek mouth, where he and his dad liked to fish, see if there were any bass hiding out in the cool spots. You didn't see a lot of bass during the day in the summer, but maybe Wendell would get lucky.

Wendell made himself two chicken sandwiches, five peanut butter and saltine crackers, wrapped five chocolate chip cookies in a napkin, and stuffed all of it into his knapsack along with the sports page, his new comic book, and a jar full of water from the pitcher in the refrigerator. The sack was on the heavy side when he hoisted it over his shoulder, but it would be light as air on the walk back, when Wendell was more likely to feel the weight of things.

The backyard stretched out for half an acre behind the house and then met up with the woods in a give-and-take of grass and weeds and spindly pines, before surrendering completely to trees and a tangled undergrowth of vines and ferns and low-lying bushes. The path through the woods stayed clear in all seasons, pounded out over years and years by human feet setting off on hikes and fishing trips. Wendell whistled for King, his redbone coonhound.

"You're a good boy," Wendell told the dog,

who took the compliment in stride, his nose sniffing the air, alert to the wide range of smells and stinks that the woods put forth every new day. Wendell didn't say anything else, aware that the dog was preoccupied, but later he would start making observations, asking King questions and waiting a respectable period of time for answers. He had a habit of doing this and hadn't even realized it until George overheard him once and asked, "You know that dog don't actually talk, right?"

Sure, Wendell knew it, but that didn't stop him now from asking, "I wonder if there really is an old cabin back in the woods? You think we'd have come across it, wouldn't you?"

King seemed to consider this, seemed almost on verge of a reply, when his ears raised up in that way that let Wendell know some other animal was nearby. King put his nose in the air and sniffed it, then let out a low growl.

"What is it, boy?" Wendell kneeled down and looked around, but there wasn't anything there that he could see. King's growl bottomed out into the lower notes of a bay and then rose into a clip of staccato barks. Wendell could sense he was waiting to be released, that every muscle in King's body was telling him to go after whatever was out there, but Wendell held back on giving the command. More than once King had reappeared after a hunt with a mangled rabbit in his mouth, and not always a dead one. If it wasn't dead, then Wendell would have to kill it to end its suffering. He wasn't so weak stomached that he couldn't do it, but it made him feel lousy for the rest of the day.

"Let's leave it, boy," Wendell told King. He started walking again, but King didn't follow him right away, so he said "Leave it" again, and then King followed him.

He thought that maybe when he got to the river, he'd find Ray Sanders or Will Cortland hanging around, fishing or just throwing rocks. But there wasn't anybody at the river when Wendell got there, and for a minute he couldn't think of what to do next. He found the rock with the flat place for sitting, took his sandwiches out of his knapsack, and started mapping out the woods in his mind. They ran for miles and miles along the southern edge of town and the countryside east and west of it, so maybe he ought to mark out the spots he'd already explored. He realized there were plenty of spots close by he'd never set foot on, since he tended to stay on the path to avoid the poison ivy. Wendell hated poison ivy worse than anything in the world and would walk a mile out of his way to avoid it.

King barked a friendly bark. Wendell looked up and saw the old yellow dog making its way toward them. The dog had been wandering around the river for a week or so now, but nobody knew who he belonged to. Every time Wendell came down, he'd see him sniffing the banks, up this way and down that way.

"Hey, boy," he called out, and the dog gave a muffled bark in response. Wendell wished he had something to give him that a dog might like, a piece of rawhide or a hard biscuit. The dog looked well fed enough, but he gave out the feeling of needing more.

King ran up to him, and the two dogs sniffed at each other a bit, noses first, then rear ends.

Then the yellow dog walked over to Wendell and let him pet him some before he went on his way.

When that colored girl showed up a few minutes later asking if that yellow dog had been around, it surprised Wendell. It surprised him even more when she said she wouldn't mind an indoor dog. It had never occurred to him that colored folks kept pets. He'd seen some dogs tied up in the yards down in the Bottom, the colored part of town, but he'd figured they were there for protection.

On the path back up through the woods, he kept thinking about that girl and why she might be interested in the yellow dog. He wondered if she was like his sister Rosemary, crazy about all dogs, oohing and aahing if she saw one with its head sticking out of a car window or moseying down the street. Rosemary had even gotten bit once by a cocker spaniel that was a lot less friendly than it looked, but that didn't stop her from loving every dog on God's green earth.

He decided to veer off the path a little bit,

just in case the cabin was close by but easily missed by a person who might avoid the thicker part of the woods because it was overgrown with poison ivy vines. He'd just keep his eyes open wide and his arms close to his sides so he wouldn't accidentally brush against anything that would make itchy rashes break out all over his skin.

He'd only gone about ten steps when, out of nowhere, that old yellow dog appeared right in front of him, barked once, and trotted off again. Wendell stopped short. All of a sudden things seemed to be connecting—the dog, the colored girl, his looking for the cabin. Maybe that old dog lived in the cabin and maybe that girl knew where the cabin was, and if she helped him find the cabin, then he'd help her find the dog.

There wasn't one thing to do but go back and get that girl.

6

How the Cabin
Became Home

Jim didn't know how he'd gotten to the cabin, and most mornings it took him a few minutes to remember where he was. Where was his Cincinnati Reds pennant? The Dutch Masters cigar box that held his arrowhead collection? Where was the blue-and-white quilt Granny had given him that time he had chicken pox in first grade? Then the chinks between the cabin's logs would come into focus, and he'd see the sunlight streaming through the cracks around the door and remember he wasn't in his room at home anymore.

Sometimes Jim felt like he'd been here before, but no memory ever rose up to tell him when that might have been, so he figured it must be the sort of place you read about in books, making it seem familiar. Could've been a hundred years old, from the looks of it, an Abe Lincoln sort of cabin with splintery, wide-planked floors and a crumbled stone fireplace. When he came back to it after roaming around in the woods or through town, it felt like home. Some days he pretended he was a grown man who'd decided on a life in the woods, away from civilization. He felt better acting like he had a choice about where he lived, when it didn't seem to him he had a choice about anything at all anymore.

Coming inside after seeing Wendell and King in the woods, he took a seat in the rickety rocking chair by the fireplace. One of the strangest things about the cabin was that somebody had carved the name Jim on the wall next to the door with a rock or a pocketknife. Sometimes it spooked him to see it, like the cabin had known before he even got there that he was coming. But other times he liked it. His name on the wall made the cabin his own.

It killed him that he couldn't clean out that fireplace. Killed him that he even wanted to, since scooping ashes from the wood-burning stove had been one of his least favorite chores back home, and it killed him that no matter how hard he tried, he couldn't pick up the small black shovel resting against the wall to do the job.

You can't build a fire without matches anyway, Jim told himself, and heard Fred's voice instead of his own. His brother was as practical as a ruler, didn't have any of Jim's dreaminess, was always looking for the straightest line from here to there. That's why he and Jim had fought so much, Jim reckoned, even though they weren't down and dirty fights. Just yelling, mostly. *I'm the big brother,* Fred liked to say, *and I am here to set an example. You listen to me, son, and I'll set you on the right path.*

Jim smiled to himself, thinking about it, seeing Fred clear as day in his droopy khaki pants and work boots, a denim shirt buttoned up all the way to the top. Farmer Fred, Jim used to tease him, and Fred always wanted to know what was so bad about being a farmer—hadn't Trebbles always been farmers, and didn't their daddy get up two hours earlier than he had to every morning so he could drive out to Uncle Owen's to check fences before he went to his law office in town?

Now you boys quit that fussing and do your chores.

Jim didn't even bother turning his head at the sound of Mama's voice. Oh, when it had first started, not all that long ago, the voices coming at him from nowhere—Mama's, Daddy's, and Fred's, Uncle Owen's and Aunt Margaret's— he'd gotten as excited as a three-year-old at Christmas. It had been a bad dream after all, he'd told himself, turning this way and that, eager to see his family and have a good laugh. *You wouldn't believe it*, he'd tell everybody, *but I had this dream where I was almost invisible and didn't have a shadow and I couldn't find any of y'all anywhere.*

Now he knew better. Wasn't nothing but

his memory playing a trick on him, putting on a play behind a curtain Jim couldn't find, no matter how hard he looked.

There was one voice, though, that he didn't recognize. He heard it almost every night, a child's voice, a boy's, coming to him from the middle of the cabin when he was lying on the cot in the corner, drifting into that strange sleep of his where he never once dreamed.

You here to carry me 'cross?

Jim squirmed in his seat, not liking to think of that voice. Wasn't scary so much as—well, Jim didn't know what. He just didn't like it that the voice seemed to know who he was. *What* he was.

Jim thought about going and waiting for Wendell to come back from the river instead of heading into town to make his daily rounds, always hoping to find his house, to see Mama and Daddy and Fred. Walking alongside Wendell, listening to him talk to King, it was like having a friend, even though it seemed weird to call a kid you'd never met a friend. Even weirder, he guessed, since Wendell didn't know Jim existed. But Jim couldn't be picky, not in his current situation, anyway. Besides, he thought he and Wendell *would* be friends, if they ever met.

Maybe today would be the day he'd work up the courage to follow Wendell home. He'd hang back in the shadows, read comic books over Wendell's shoulder, watch Wendell's mama put supper on the table while Wendell played a game of Monopoly with his sisters or worked a jigsaw puzzle. He'd listen at the window for the sound of Mr. Crow's truck pulling into the drive.

Now there was a sound he missed—a truck pulling into a gravel driveway at suppertime.

Come on, boys, and tell your mama to put supper on the back burner, we got work to do in the fields!

Soon as they heard their daddy's voice, him and Fred would fly out to the truck and jump in back, Mama standing at the porch waving a spoon at Daddy, yelling about how he was ruining another supper of hers, but laughing, too, because she knew how much Daddy loved that farm he worked with Uncle Owen. Daddy would back that truck up so fast the engine whined like a tornado wind.

No. He wouldn't go to Wendell's today. He had to find Daddy and Fred. And Mama. That was his job now. If he could only find them and let them know he was still here, well, maybe they could help him come home.

7

A Brief History of Celeste, Kentucky

For such a small town Celeste, Kentucky, was prouder than you might think it had a right to be. Still, it *had* been home to General Flavius McCarver, Revolutionary War hero, who walked along these sidewalks as a boy, back when they were made out of wooden boards. Everyone in Celeste knew about General McCarver. Any day of the week you could see him in the intersection of Main and River Streets, sitting upright upon his stone horse, one arm pointed straight ahead, like he'd been sent by God to direct traffic.

Celeste, Kentucky, was proud of all sorts of things. It was proud of its brand-new school, Thomas Edison Elementary, on Green Street, and of its high school's outstanding marching band, the Fighting Bear Cats, which had placed third in the North Central Kentucky Regional Finals two years in a row, and it was very, very proud of Marjorie Holder, the Fighting Bear Cats' drum majorette, who was arguably the most beautiful majorette in all of Kentucky, or at least in the tricounty area.

But Celeste, like any small town, had its secrets. For instance, only a few of the townspeople knew that the business offices of Felts Paper Products had been built on the remains of an Indian mound. The mound was discovered by the site foreman fifteen minutes after the ground had been broken to begin building. Work was stopped, the mayor was notified, a rushed committee meeting was held. All in attendance agreed the public did not need to be informed, despite the fact that the local paper, the *Celeste Gazette and Informer*, had recently run a well-received editorial saying that the mounds in their area should be respected and preserved.

Celeste had even bigger secrets than that. The runaway slaves who'd made their way soundlessly through the woods to the river-bank at night were such a secret that hardly anyone in the white part of town knew about them or would ever know about them. When you crossed over to the colored part of town, which was generally considered to begin east of the intersection of South Central and Lexington and ran all the way down Marigold Lane before it stopped abruptly at the woods near the river, the secret was common cur-rency. You might have been in the kitchen help-ing your grandmother make biscuits when she told you about her own grandmother rocking slowly on the porch in her old age—the age of remembering—and whistling *whippoorwill, whippoorwill* under her breath and then whis-pering, "Friend of a friend, friend of a friend."

Callie Robinson's grandmother, Mama Lou,

was one who remembered the stories her grandmother had told about the refugees on their way north under the dark of night, and she'd passed them on to her granddaughter. Now, as Callie followed the boy with the red dog up the path from the river, trying to avoid the tendrils of poison ivy climbing every tree she passed, she wondered if she was walking over the same ground the escaped slaves had walked over. Wouldn't that be something?

She wanted to tap the boy on the shoulder and ask if he knew the stories about the slaves coming through Celeste on their way to getting free, but she didn't think she ought to talk to white folks about that kind of thing. It was too good a story just to hand over to any old body, especially some boy whose name she didn't even know. Who knew what he might do with it—make fun, say it never happened, tell that old lie that some white folks liked, about how happy slaves had been.

So instead she asked him about the yellow dog. "You got any guesses where he come from? That dog, I mean? Somebody around here must have owned him sometime. Otherwise, why would he be here?"

"I've been thinking on that," the boy said, holding up a branch of a bush for her to duck under before letting it whip back, which made Callie all the more sure he wasn't planning on beating her with a stick. "I reckon he's on the prowl for something or somebody. But I don't know anybody who knows him."

"He's a pretty old dog," Callie said. "Maybe somebody owned him back in the day. Maybe his folks lived upriver. Could be they all died of a fever and he's been on his own ever since."

"But why would he come down here if his folks lived upriver?"

"Could've got lonely," Callie guessed. "Or confused."

"Maybe," Wendell said. "Maybe he's like one of them dogs you read about sometimes that get lost on a camping trip and find their way back home."

"Pretty old dog to take camping."

"Maybe the folks who took him camping

were old too," Wendell said, and then he stopped and pointed to a broken-off stump of a tree and stopped walking. "That dog was right around here. You smell him, King?"

As if to answer, King gave a sharp bark and trotted to where the path branched right. The boy followed him, and Callie followed the boy. King barked again, and this time an answering bark came from close by. "Come on out, pup," the boy called. "Come on an' see us now."

And sure enough, didn't that old yellow dog show up right in front of them, wagging his tail and sniffing at King? Callie kneeled down beside him and scratched him behind his ears. "Where you gone off to, boy? I been needing you to tell me a thing or two." She looked up. "How old you reckon he is?"

The boy considered this. "Pretty old, I guess. Look at that white fur around his eyes. That's a sign of age."

Callie stood and brushed the dirt off her knees. "What's your name, anyway? I been meaning to ask you that for about a hundred years now."

"Wendell Crow," the boy said, grinning at the "hundred years" remark. "What's yours?"

"I'm Callie Robinson." She stuck out her hand. "I'm pleased to meet you."

Wendell looked at her hand like he wasn't sure what he was supposed to do with it, but after a moment's hesitation he shook. "I've got some cousins named Robinson, but I don't reckon you all are related to one another."

"No," agreed Callie. "I don't reckon so."

They stood there for a moment, considering each other, and then Wendell said, "You don't know anything about a cabin out here, do you? I mean, here in the woods? My dad says he remembers one."

Callie shrugged. "I might have heard tell of one," she replied, trying to sound casual about it. Oh, she'd heard tell of one, all right, but that didn't mean she had to pass on the information.

At least not yet.

"Well, you wanna help me look for it?"

"You think it's gonna help me find something out about this dog?"

"Might could," Wendell said. "You don't know till you find out, I guess."

True enough. "Come on," she said to the yellow dog, who obediently followed her as she started off again up the path. "Let's go find us a cabin."

The Woods

Wendell wondered how long it would take to find the cabin. What if his dad was wrong, and it wasn't anywhere near the Jerichos' farm? His dad had plenty of stories about how far he and his brothers had roamed when they were boys. He claimed that one day they'd followed the river all the way to Covington, fifteen miles north, taken a quick look around town, then walked all the way back and gotten home before nightfall.

That made Wendell think. If they didn't find the cabin today, maybe he could ride his bike over to Uncle James's house after dinner. Uncle James was the oldest of his dad's brothers, and the one whose head rested most squarely upon his shoulders. His other uncles, Phillip and Edsel, couldn't tell a story straight if you paid them to, and his dad could be the same way, stretching out a fact to make it just a little more colorful than it needed to be. Uncle James might thump his Bible a little harder than Wendell cared for, but he could be trusted to tell the truth.

Wouldn't it be something when Wendell went home and told his dad he'd found the cabin? He could just about see his dad's face, all proud and excited. That tired look would fall away from his eyes, and he'd grab his hat from the peg near the door. *Come on, son*, he'd say. *Show me where it is.*

"If I come home covered with poison ivy, my mama's gonna wonder what I been up to," the girl, Callie, said from behind him. "She'll fuss and fuss."

Then Wendell had a funny thought. Did colored folks use calamine lotion when they got a rash? And if they did, did it look funny, all that pink against their dark skin? Well, the pink looked pretty strange against his white skin, that was the truth.

"My mother makes me take a bath in oatmeal when I get poison ivy," Wendell said. "Yours ever do that? It helps, but I still can't sleep at night from all the itching."

"The first thing Mama does is rub you all over with alcohol, to cool your skin down. And then she makes this nasty paste out of baking soda that she plasters all over you, and you just have to sit there and let it dry. Makes you feel like a mummy or something."

"Yeah, my mom does that if we get a mosquito bite. Only she just puts it on the bite. It sort of helps."

The problem with talking about itching, Wendell realized, was that it made you feel itchy whether you had any cause to or not. He scratched at his neck and then his left arm. Poison ivy was practically dripping from the trees around him, and he was doing his best not to rub up against it, but maybe his mother was right. Maybe Wendell could get a rash by just standing next to some poison ivy. He didn't even need to touch it.

They reached a fork in the path. King and the old yellow dog sniffed the air, first to the left and then to the right. The part of the path that veered left was worn and well traveled; to the right you could barely see any path at all, but it was there, hidden under the leaves. King looked back at Wendell, waiting for a command. Wendell turned to Callie. "I reckon we ought to go toward the right. It looks like it'll take us deeper into the woods. I'm pretty sure if we go left, we're going to be heading up to the Jerichos' farm."

Callie looked worried. "We gonna be able to get back out of these woods? Maybe we ought to mark our way."

"King will get us out," Wendell said, feeling proud about it. "He always knows the way back."

So they followed the path deeper into the woods, Wendell doing his best to avoid the ivy vines, even as the trees closed more tightly around them. He wished he were a bird flying overhead so he could see exactly where they were. He could still smell the river air, the muddy stink of it.

But there were other smells here too, the darker, damper smells of rotting leaves, moss-covered trees, and animal scat. The woods were quieter than the river, which was funny if you thought about it, since all sorts of wild things lived here, not to mention insects. Of course, if you wanted to hear the woods get noisy, you had to come at night. Once or twice in the summer Wendell and his dad came down this way to fish at night, and critters made so much racket you wanted to cover your ears.

King gave a sharp bark, as if he were making an announcement, and Wendell thought that maybe they'd found the cabin, and then he started to worry. What if Callie made a claim on the cabin, said that it was half hers? It might be she'd want to hold tea parties in it, and that would spoil the whole feel of the cabin for Wendell, even if he wasn't there when the parties took place. He remembered now why he did his best to keep away from girls. The ideas they came up with could ruin your whole day. Like the time Rosemary went on a decorating kick. When Wendell got home from his baseball game and went up to his room to change, he found half of his baseball card collection pasted to the walls. His Ted Kluszewski, his Gus Bell, his Walker Cooper, all ruined, and nobody even made Rosemary pay him back. "She was just trying to be nice," his mother said, like good intentions made up for the destruction of personal property. That was female logic for you right there.

The path just kept rambling on, not leading toward any place in particular, it seemed to Wendell. He'd thought heading away from the Jerichos' farm was the right idea, but the fact was he didn't know this part of the woods at all.

"I'm starting to think we ain't on the right path," Callie said, like she'd been reading Wendell's mind. Well, maybe they should call this whole thing off, he thought. Maybe Callie and the old dog weren't part of the plan after all. Could be he didn't need them to find the cabin, that they didn't have a thing to do with it.

In fact, he was starting to doubt the wisdom of including the girl on this hunt through the woods in the first place. What if they found the cabin, and the next time around, when Wendell brought his dad or George to see the place, this skinny, knobby-kneed colored girl was sitting smack in the middle of it, maybe with a few of her colored friends? "Well, hey there, Wendell," she might call out, and then he'd have to explain how he knew her. Word would get around town pretty fast if folks thought Wendell was mixing with colored kids.

Now, ain't you in a pickle? he could hear his sister Rosemary ask, and Wendell reckoned he was. He needed to do something now, and he needed to do it quick.

"I think you're right," Wendell told Callie, turning around to face her. "I don't think this is the way at all. I guess we best go back."

"Then let's try another path," Callie suggested. "Wouldn't take long to retrace our steps, take the other fork in the road."

"I—I need to get going home," Wendell stammered. "Got chores to do."

Callie gave him a long look. "You had all the time in the world before. How'd you get so busy all of a sudden?"

Wendell was opening his mouth to reply when something thudded on the ground behind him.

"Don't move." Callie held out a hand and took a few steps toward him. King let out a low growl, and the old yellow dog whimpered. "There's a snake behind you. It just fell out of a tree, like it meant to block your path. I ain't never seen anything like it."

"What kind of snake?" Wendell asked, his whole body going cold. He could tolerate a lot of things, but a snake wasn't one of them.

"Reckon it's a black snake," Callie said, peering over Wendell's shoulder. "It ain't moving. Must have gotten stunned by the fall. You don't reckon it jumped, do you?"

Wendell darted over to King and turned around. A thick black snake lay two feet behind where he'd been standing. Callie was right,

74

though. It wasn't moving or acting like it was all that alive.

Callie inched closer to the creature. "I'd say that was a black snake, all right. Every once in a while one slips into our basement, and I'm the only one who don't mind to carry it out. Black snakes won't hurt you. You want to touch it?"

To Wendell's amazement, Callie leaned down and grabbed the snake by its middle. It wriggled in her hand, tongue flickering, its head shifting this way and that, like it was considering who it should kill first. She held it out to him, and Wendell automatically took three steps back.

"Snakes give you the willies?" Callie asked. "I don't know what the fuss is, myself. Now, if it was a copperhead, I'd be a mile gone already. But this here fella wouldn't hurt a fly."

"That snake's a sign," Wendell said, gathering his wits. He needed to use this situation to his advantage. "I think I've read it in a book somewhere. Snake falls in your path, go the other way. In fact, you probably should just give up and go home."

"You sure are superstitious, Wendell Crow." Callie shook her head and dropped the snake to the ground, where it slithered back into the underbrush. "Well, I reckon we'll just have to start our journey back up in the morning, what with snakes falling from trees and you having chores to do."

Wendell tried to think fast. "You know, I'm starting to think there might not even be a cabin. We're probably wasting our time."

"Oh, there's a cabin, all right," Callie said. "Sure as you and me are standing here, there's a cabin. I aim to find it too. Maybe that's where this old dog stays. But you can give up looking if you want to. Nobody'd blame you a bit, what with all the snakes and poison ivy around here."

"I ain't giving up." Wendell turned to King and snapped his fingers. "Come on, boy, let's head home."

"Tell you what," Callie said from behind him as they started walking. "You don't have to even come looking tomorrow. I'm happy to be the lone explorer out here. I'll let you know if I find anything, you have my word."

"I'll meet you at the river, nine o'clock sharp," Wendell said. He shook his head. What a mess. What in the world had he been thinking about, getting involved with this girl? Well, it was too late to do anything about it now. He'd just focus on the main point. He'd just think about how happy his dad would be if Wendell found the cabin, no matter how many knobby-kneed colored girls were trying to lay claim to it.

After ten minutes of walking Wendell could see a widening up ahead and reckoned they were almost back at the big path leading up from the river. Maybe if he and Callie found the cabin tomorrow, he could bring his dad on Sunday. His dad might tell him some more stories about his growing-up days. The best days of his life, he called them. Wendell loved hearing those stories, but he always wished that right now was his dad's best time. Once, he'd heard his mother say, "I can hardly remember life before the children were born." His dad never said anything like that.

9

Thomas; or, The Other Boy Who Lived in the Cabin

He'd watched that ghosty boy tracing over those letters on the wall with his ghosty finger and heard him say "Jim" every time he did, like he be calling out for somebody. Thomas didn't know no letters except for *X*, so how he supposed to write his name and let folks know he still here? He been trying to tell that ghosty boy ever since he shown up here, but the ghosty boy wouldn't listen. Thomas stood next to him at night and said, Listen to me! Said, Let me tell you something! And then he tell the ghosty boy the whole story, even if that boy act like he don't hear a word.

He'd say, Me and my folks and all the rest of them was coming down the path through the woods at night when we heard the hounds, and then that man guiding us say, *Go to the cabin, hide there till it's safe. They's a place to hide under the floor, and the old lady, she'll tell them catcher mens to go away.*

So then we got to this place and climbed through a hole in the floor and we was hiding and it smelled like dirt and damp and there was things crawling on me and then there was a skinny ole snake just slithering toward me—couldn't see it, but I could hear it!—and I just set out to yelling and yelling and they was all saying, *Thomas! Stop! Hush! Them mens gonna hear you!*

But I just couldn't stop. That snake was crawling closer, and it was gonna slide into my ear, I just knowed it. I just had to yell and scream, and then Big Charles come right beside me and said, *Sweet Jesus, forgive me,* and he pull me to his side, and at first I felt all safe and good, 'cause Big Charles be the biggest one of all, and weren't no snake gonna crawl into my ear with Big Charles near me. But then Big Charles pulled me into him so that my mouth be all covered up and I tried to suck in some air, but I couldn't find any anywhere.

Well, didn't take too long for little stars to start dancing across my eyes, and then it be black as night for a long, long time, until one day I just sort of rose up outta that hole, but weren't nobody here.

You the first one who stayed any amount of time, Thomas always told the ghosty boy. I been thinking maybe they sent you to carry me across the river, so I can meet my folks on the other side. But you don't say nothing. You never even asked if you could be here. Just showed up like this your place. I don't mind to share it, but why won't you act like you know I'm here too? Just turn around? Just say hello?

That ghosty boy, well, it was like somebody hit him from behind whenever Thomas said that. So why wouldn't he turn around? Why wouldn't he just for once turn around and say hey?

10

Company Comes
to the Woods

Voices woke Jim up the next morning, one familiar, the other strange. The strange voice belonged to a girl. The voice he knew was Wendell's. They were a little ways off, not in the clearing yet, still in the woods, but getting closer. Sort of felt to Jim like he had company coming, and he jumped out of bed, wishing he could straighten things up, set out some chairs.

"I'm getting eat up alive by no-see-ums," the girl said. "Don't recall it being so buggy out here yesterday."

"Rained last night," Wendell replied. "The rain brings out the bugs."

"Well, between the bites and the poison ivy, I ain't gonna be nothing but one big itch. You think we're headed in the right direction?"

"What other direction is there? We already found the wrong direction yesterday."

King barked sharply, and the girl cried, "Look now, over there! Woods open up over there."

Standing at the window by the door, Jim could hear the rustling of branches being pushed aside.

"We better make something clear right now," Jim heard Wendell say, and the rustling stopped. "If we find the cabin, you can't be bringing your friends over here for tea parties. It ain't gonna be that kind of place."

"Who gave you the right to say what kind of place it is or it ain't?" the girl asked. "It don't belong to you."

"Don't belong to you, either."

"Maybe we ought to find it before we start arguing about ownership."

The girl broke into the clearing first. Probably eleven or twelve, Jim thought. Skinny, her
hair pulled into two short braids. "Look! It's
back there! Ain't nothing but a falling-down
thing, either."

Wendell emerged from the woods into the
clearing. He stood for a minute, studying the
cabin, nodding like he had a big plan. "Yeah,
but you can see how somebody could have
lived there. Might could live there still. All it
needs is a few repairs."

"More than a few," the girl said, and then
she started trembling, like the excitement of
seeing the cabin was an electric current under
her skin. "We found it."

"You think we ought to go inside?" Wendell
asked, his voice quieter now, more cautious. The
girl nodded, and Wendell took the lead, even
though there wasn't much of a path to the cabin
and the poison ivy vines were everywhere.

"Don't think just because you touch the
door first that you have claim to this cabin,"
the girl said, close on Wendell's heels. "You
remember that, now."

"You're gonna drive me crazy. I ain't trying to claim anything."

The girl harrumphed. "We'll see what we see."

Jim felt suddenly embarrassed that the door to the cabin didn't have a knob or a latch. There was a hole in it where a knob might have been, a place where maybe you'd string a rope through and pull the door to after you'd gone inside. Wendell was about to push the door in with his shoulder when the girl stopped him.

"I ain't sure we should do this," she said. She stood about five feet back, still with a tremble in her voice. "We might be—well, disturbing something."

"Nobody lives here," Wendell insisted. "It ain't livable. Look at that roof. The place must flood every time it rains."

"I ain't talking about people."

"Then what are you talking about? Squirrels?"

The girl hesitated. "Now, don't get me wrong, but every place has got some life in it, even if ain't no one living there. You got to be respectful."

84

"I'll be respectful," Wendell promised, pushing open the door. "Cold in here. Smells like smoke."

Jim backed away from the window. He went and stood over by the fireplace, his back flat against the wall.

"That fireplace is made from fieldstones," the girl said, following Wendell inside. "That's why it's held up so good. Why you reckon it's cold in here? Hot enough day outside."

Wendell shrugged. "I don't know. It's not like it's shut up tight." He pointed to the corner, where the roof seemed to have partially collapsed without dropping all the way in. "And that window don't have glass. You'd think the air in here would be the same as it is on the outside."

He walked with care across the floor, testing the planks with his weight. "Floor seems solid enough. What do you reckon that is?" Wendell pointed to the corner. "You think that's a bed frame?"

"Yeah, I reckon it is," the girl said. "See how them pieces of rope is strung from one side to the other? You could pile some quilts across them, for a kind of bed."

She walked to the fireplace. "Look at this old black shovel. Bet it's a hundred years old at least." She wrapped her arms around herself and gave an exaggerated shiver. "This place sure has got a strange feel to it. Maybe that's why your dog didn't follow us in."

Wendell walked over to the door and looked out. "Come here, King! Everything's okay, boy. Come on in and sniff around."

Jim peered out the door. King was giving Wendell a long look that said he wasn't coming inside anytime soon.

"Hey!" the girl called. "Look at this!"

When Wendell turned around, the girl was pointing to the wall next to the door.

"This cabin belongs to somebody named Jim," she declared. "His name's written right here."

Wendell took a look. "Yeah, it says 'Jim,' all right. Looks like someone carved it with some sort of knife. Fishing knife, maybe. Maybe the cabin belonged to somebody named Jim a long time ago."

"Maybe, maybe not. This cabin has a mysterious feel to it, you got to admit. Who knows who's hanging around?"

Wendell snorted. "Buncha bats hanging around, probably. A few possums. I don't think there's anything mysterious here."

"Then why won't your dog come in? I'll tell you why. He's feeling the same thing I am. Like this is somebody else's place."

Wendell nodded thoughtfully. "Maybe you're right. We ought to get out of here, in case they come back. We don't want to be trespassers."

Jim smiled. He could tell from the sound of Wendell's voice he had every plan on coming back, only the next time he was coming by himself, or maybe with some buddies. Jim liked the idea of that. Things sure would feel less lonely if a gang of boys started hanging out around here.

"Yeah, we ought to get out of here," the girl agreed. "And then you know what we ought to do? We ought to see if we can find something about this old Jim. I'm putting that on the top of my list of things to research."

"Good idea." Wendell turned toward the door and stuck his hand outside. "I'll admit it's strange how cold it is in here, and it's strange King won't come in. Probably a hundred things to explain that, though. Probably another old black snake curled up in the eaves. Nothing to be afraid of."

The girl snorted. "Nothing to be afraid of at all about an old black snake."

Wendell reddened, and Jim wondered why.

"Let's go, boy," Wendell called to King as he stepped out of the cabin, the girl following him, and then Jim. King rose on all fours and put his nose up into the air. He let out a short bark, and another dog barked in response.

Jim stopped. The hairs on his arms prickled, or at least that's how it felt in his mind, like his every last nerve had gone taut.

"Hey, old dog," the girl called out. "We been wondering where you were."

An old dog, a golden retriever, made his way slowly into the clearing, turning his head this way and that, sniffing the air and letting out a whine.

"What's wrong?" the girl asked him. "Something don't smell right to you? Well, it's a strange place, I admit."

She reached out to touch the dog, but Wendell stopped her, saying, "Let him be. He's onto something."

The retriever had white fur around his eyes, and his movements were slow and a little unsure.

Buddy, Jim whispered. How'd you get so old?

The dog's whine grew louder, and he began to run in circles, still sniffing the air, still looking this way and that.

"What's he going on about?" the girl asked. "You don't think he's got rabies, do you?"

"I don't know," Wendell said. "It's the strangest thing I've ever seen."

Jim took a few steps toward his dog. I'm right here, boy. I know you know it. You just can't see me. Come on now, boy. Come here.

And Buddy came right up to him, sniffed

89

the air, and then walked away. Jim sank to the ground and put his head in his hands. He felt the hope he'd been holding on to—the hope that he'd find his family, the hope that everything could be made right—slip out of him. Even his own dog didn't know him.

A breath brushed against his ear. Jim looked up. Buddy stood next to him, still whining a bit, still looking around. But he was there, planted firmly on the ground.

Wendell whistled and said, "Come on now, pup. We're heading back."

"Looks like that old dog wants to stay here," the girl said. "Keep an eye on the place."

"Let him, I guess."

"I guess."

You're a good boy, Buddy, Jim said softly, leaning against his dog's shoulder. He hoped against hope that Buddy could feel him.

Buddy whined again and then stretched out on the ground. Jim scratched him between his ears and heard the old dog sigh.

11

Mysteries and Secrets

Callie had a whole bunch of mysteries to solve, and she didn't know where to start. She had secrets filling up her pockets, and she didn't know who she should tell. That cabin was a secret, except folks in the Bottom had known about it forever. Maybe they didn't talk about it, and maybe most of them didn't know exactly where it was, but they knew the stories. Sometimes a preacher would preach about it. He'd lean over the pulpit and say, *Our people have always been strong!*

And the ladies would wave their fans and

say, *Uh-huh, that's right*, and the men would nod and say, *Amen, Preacher.*

The preacher'd say, *Our people ran through the darkness, down to the River Jordan, and they swam across to freedom. They were* strong *men and* strong *women.*

Uh-huh, uh-huh, that's right, amen.

They had a desire to be free, and God made them free, and God will make you free too, if you let Him.

A teacher might teach about it, and more than one mother had scared her children away from the woods at night by saying, *Them woods haunted, that's what I hear. Slave catcher's ghost still roaming. Still looking for little colored children hid away in there.*

But that boy Wendell? Callie was pretty sure he didn't know that cabin was anything more than an old, falling-down place that somebody lived in a long time ago. You could ask Wendell Crow about runaway slaves crossing the river, and Callie bet his eyes would pop right out. He might ask, *Here in Kentucky? Weren't no slaves in this part of Kentucky*, he might say.

That's because the Bottom started out as a

freeman's settlement, Callie would have told him. *Founded by free people of color*. Her people. She wondered if Wendell knew about that, or if that was one more important fact that white folks let slip by them.

That was a thing that bothered her, Callie thought as she walked along the riverbed back toward home. She felt like she knew everything there was to know about white folks. She knew all their facts and famous people. She knew where the white children went to school and where they went to church, but she doubted if hardly any of them knew where the colored school was or that there were three different churches in the Bottom and that it made a difference which one you went to. You never saw white children walking around the Bottom. It was like they lacked curiosity, Callie thought. How could you live in the same town as other people and not want to know about them?

She climbed up the path from the river, and pretty soon she was back at Mrs. Kendall's yard, and there the old lady was, sitting on a rickety old stool in front of her tomatoes. It sounded like she was singing. Well, Callie had heard of stranger things people did to get their gardens to grow. She wished her own garden didn't grow so many weeds, and she wished she had something better to do than getting back to the house to finish weeding before Mama got home from work.

Well, maybe she *did* have something better to do, come to think of it. Wouldn't take her but five minutes to get to the *Weekly Advance*'s office, and Mr. Renfrow, who'd been the editor for over twenty years, he knew just about everything there was to know about Celeste, Kentucky. He knew about colored folks and white folks. He knew about the Indian mounds on the outskirts of town and about the Indians that built them. Once, Mr. Renfrow had come to school to tell the students about the people who had lived on this land way before anybody else—the Adena people, followed by the Hopewells, and then the Shawnee.

If anybody in Celeste could help Callie solve her mysteries, that person was Mr. Orin Renfrow.

The *Weekly Advance* office was housed on Lexington Street, right next to Shirley's Grocery and down two spots from the Laundromat. It had a big plate-glass window with THE WEEKLY ADVANCE written in fancy letters across it, and under that the words EDITOR: ORIN P. RENFROW. When you looked through the window, you could see a counter with a little bell ringer on it, and a half-dead ficus tree dripping brown leaves all over the floor. When Callie pushed the door open, she was greeted by the sound of Mr. Renfrow's typewriter going *rat-a-tat-tat*. He was the fastest typer she knew, even though he only used two fingers.

"Good afternoon, Miss Callie," Mr. Renfrow called, not bothering to look up. "You come to pay your bill? It's not due until Friday."

Callie walked up to the counter and peered over it to Mr. Renfrow's messy desk. "How'd you know it was me? You didn't even lift up your eyes when I walked in."

"I have excellent peripheral vision. Always have. How's your mama?"

"She's still pretty, if that's what you're

wondering." Callie had a suspicion that Mr. Renfrow was sweet on her mama, but who could blame him for that? It didn't worry her none, seeing as her daddy was a tall and handsome man, and Mr. Renfrow was already wrinkled and gray.

Mr. Renfrow typed a few more words, then swiveled in his chair so that he was facing Callie. "Happy to hear it. Now, little Miss Callie, how may I help you?"

"I'm trying to figure something out," Callie told him, "but I ain't sure what it is. Or else it's a bunch of things. Like this old yellow dog that's been wandering around town. I've been wondering who he belongs to. You know that dog?"

Mr. Renfrow nodded. "I've seen him. Sometimes he spends the night over at Mrs. Kendall's, but best as I can tell, he doesn't belong to anybody."

"But he musta used to. And I got a hunch maybe he belonged to somebody named Jim. Maybe a long time ago. And maybe this Jim lived in the woods by the river, up from the big bend."

Mr. Renfrow raised an eyebrow. "And how

do you know about this somebody named Jim?"

Callie shrugged. "I hear things. You spend as much time in the front yard weeding as I do, you bound to hear folks talk as they pass by."

Mr. Renfrow stood up and walked over to the counter. "So you need to track down this Jim, who may or may not exist. Do you have a last name?"

"No, no last name." Callie leaned across the counter and lowered her voice. "Here's what I'm thinking. I think this Jim died, and this old dog is looking for him. But I also think this Jim might have died a long time ago. 'Cause if he died last week, why, folks would know about it, right? But if he died a while back, the memory of this Jim would be thin. People probably forgot all about him."

"And how do you think Jim died?"

Callie thought for a minute. "Could've drowned in the river, I reckon. Maybe he went for a swim by himself, which you ain't supposed to do. You always supposed to swim with a buddy. But maybe Jim forgot, or he got so hot one afternoon he thought he'd take a little dip by himself. Thought it wouldn't do him no harm, but he was wrong about that."

Mr. Renfrow nodded. "There've been plenty of drownings over the years, it's true. That's a hazard of living so close to a river. Folks go fishing when the water's still wild in the spring; folks get drunk and decide to take a swim. Children wander down to the water and fall in. I believe that's one reason the town council voted to build a pool, to keep children away from the river. It's an excellent idea, which is why I'm writing an editorial about it."

"But why you writing about that? Colored folks can't swim in the town pool."

"And that's exactly why I'm writing about it," Mr. Renfrow said. "The town pool was paid for with taxpayer money, and everyone in Celeste pays taxes, not just white folks."

"Well, best of luck, Mr. Renfrow," Callie said. She didn't bother to tell him he was wasting his time. That wasn't the sort of thing grown-ups liked to hear, even if it was true. First of all, white folks didn't read the *Weekly Advance*, so how were they supposed to get wind of Mr.

Renfrow's ideas? Secondly, weren't no white folks gonna let no colored folks swim in the same pool as them. You could get mad about it all you wanted, but facts were facts. "In the meantime, you know how I could get a list of all the folks that drowned in the river in the last ten years or so?"

"I can't say I have such a list on hand. You'd have to search through the archives in the basement. We've got forty years' worth of the *Advance* down there."

"Wouldn't need to look at but ten years. Maybe fifteen. Dogs don't live much past fifteen, if they live that long." Then Callie had a thought. "If Jim was white, would you have put a story about it in the paper?"

"The *Advance* reports all the news," Mr. Renfrow told her, puffing out his chest a little. "If it happens in Celeste, my readers want to read about it. Now, young lady, follow me and I'll show you the archives."

Later that afternoon, when Callie got home, her fingers were coated with ink and her hair was thick with dust. Normally, she never volunteered to take a bath, but as soon as she walked into the house, she headed straight for the tub. No way could she eat dinner with that stuff all over her hands.

"You're late!" Regina called from the sitting room. "You were supposed to be home thirty minutes ago!"

"Mama home yet?" Callie yelled back as she twisted on the tub's faucet. "'Cause if Mama's not home, then what's it to you?"

"Better hope Mama don't see them weeds!"

The weeds. Callie shook her head, sighing. It was always the dang weeds. Well, she'd just tell Mama her hands had gotten too cramped up. Maybe she was coming down with arthritis.

Sinking down into the tub, Callie closed her eyes and watched headline after headline flash across her mind. She'd only had time to go through a half a year of the *Weekly Advance*, and that half year of papers, twenty-six in all, was so stuffed with happenings and doings and living and dying that, even skimming, Callie thought it was going to take forever to finish.

Well, maybe that was because she wasn't so good at skimming. Oh, it wasn't hard when it came to town council meetings and notices about where you could dump your trash and where you couldn't, but Callie kept getting caught up in stories about club meetings and church gatherings and who had come to town to visit who.

There were meetings of the Domestic Economy Social Club and the American War Mothers convention, both held at the Baptist church on Clinton Street. The Town and Country Club met monthly in the back room of Shirley's Grocery, making plans to help the needy of the colored community. Callie knew about Town and Country because her daddy went to that, even though Mama said it was a sad day when the only way a poor man in this town could get help was by another poor man emptying out his pockets.

There was the Green Hill Baptist Church and the Corinthian Baptist Church and the Rock of Ages Seventh-Day Adventist Church, and each and every week it seemed like at least one of them was having a chicken dinner to raise money for some cause or another, war orphans or children in Africa or a new building. Callie wondered how Mr. Renfrow stayed so thin, reporting on all the church suppers the way he did. She knew there was no way he'd be let out the door without a dozen women handing him plates of chicken and dumplings and sweet potato biscuits and bowl after bowl of greens swimming in pot likker.

Just reading about all that good food had made Callie hungry. She had been lingering over a description of Mrs. Pauline Johnson's double-chocolate cake ("My secret ingredient is pepper," Mrs. Johnson had divulged to Mr. Renfrow. "Just a pinch. It livens a cake up") when she realized that at this rate it would probably take her five years of reading to get through ten years of papers.

Now, sinking down into the tub, Callie decided that tomorrow she'd start at the beginning—1943 instead of 1953—and then work her way back up to the present times. She reckoned she'd been right, that if Jim had drowned in the river in the last couple of years, people would have a better memory of it. No, it had to have happened a ways back.

Callie wasn't sure why she felt so strongly there was a connection between the dog and the cabin and this person Jim, whose name was carved into the cabin's wall. She guessed it was the way that old dog had laid down in front of the cabin and wouldn't budge. There were a lot of little mysteries that she was hoping were all connected together, though she knew she might be chasing down a bunch of dead-end streets. But she'd gotten started, and once Callie started something, she liked to see it through all the way to the end.

Regina banged on the door. "Mama's home and fixing dinner. You better get on out of there and set the table. 'Sides, I need to use the bathroom."

"Out in a minute," Callie called, grabbing the sides of the tub and pulling herself up. "Give me a second to dry off."

"You got one second and that's it!"

Shoot, Callie thought, that Regina sure was

a mean-tempered thing. She needed to get out of the house and do something with her day, that was her problem.

What would Mama and Daddy think about how she'd spent her day, Callie wondered as she dried herself off with her favorite towel, the one with yellow daisies on it. Daddy would be mad at her for going down to the river by herself, and Mama would sputter and steam if she knew Callie had gone walking around the woods with some white boy she'd never seen before in her life. But Callie bet if she told them about finding the cabin, that would get their interest.

Who wouldn't be interested in that cabin? It was Celeste's best-kept secret, and now Callie knew where it was.

And so did Wendell Crow.

Callie hadn't given any thought to what Wendell would do next. Would he forget about it now that they'd found it? Boys could be that way, enjoying the chase more than the catch. But what if Wendell had a plan? He'd acted like he wasn't all that interested, but maybe he was thinking about—shoot, Callie didn't know—maybe he was thinking about chopping the cabin down and selling the pieces for firewood. Maybe he was going to light it on fire and dance all around it. Maybe he was going to turn it into a private place where only he and his friends could go.

She decided she better put Wendell Crow on her list of mysteries that needed to be figured out.

"Callie!" Now Carl Jr. was pounding on the door. Dang, people, couldn't a girl have half a minute to put some clothes on? "Come on out, Callie!"

"Hold your horses! I'm getting dressed!"

"Well, hurry up," Carl Jr. called through the door. "Mr. Renfrow's on the front porch, and he says he's got something to show you."

12

Seeing Fred

Fred had hardly ever come to town, not that Jim could remember. When he wasn't in school, he'd been at Uncle Owen's farm doing chores. Soon as Fred got his driver's license, Uncle Owen had hired him as a hand, and Fred's dinner-table talk was always full of birthing calves and curing tobacco and whether or not Uncle Owen ought to trade his team of horses in for a tractor.

But now Jim felt almost positive that he saw Fred talking to a man outside of McKinley's Drug. Only this Fred looked old. Not old-man old, but grown-up old. Jim tried to remember the last time he'd seen his brother. Could've been years, he supposed. Had it been long enough for Fred to finish growing up? Jim didn't like the thought of that—that Fred had kept getting older while Jim had just stopped.

Fred, he called, but his voice came out the way it always did these days, like a thin rope of wind curling around the branches of a tree. No sound to it at all. Jim wondered if there was something he could do to bring his voice back. He'd read an article once about a baseball umpire who did special exercises to make his voice carry farther. Something about breathing in deep down to your stomach, then exhaling like there was a tube running from your insides to your outsides. Problem was, Jim didn't exactly breathe anymore. Or if he did, he couldn't figure out how he was doing it.

Maybe if he walked right up to Fred and stood next to him. If anybody would know him, it would be Fred, Jim figured. Who was closer to you than your own brother?

"Elizabeth's set on us going to Louisville for

the weekend," Fred was telling the man beside him. "Says we won't have time to go anywhere when the tobacco comes in."

"She's right about that, I reckon," the man said, and then he clapped Fred on the shoulder. "Course, you take her to Louisville, you might spend your tobacco crop before you get it to market."

Fred laughed, and Jim was surprised by how much it was a grown man's laugh, full and hearty. "You got that right, son. And she says she just needs one new dress, but I've heard that before, and every time she comes home with three."

Jim stood as close to Fred as he could without touching him. He wished he could still smell things instead of just remembering how they smelled. Fred had always smelled like cedar pencils and the dry autumn leaves, with a sweet little tang of cow manure right around the edges.

"Well, I reckon I ought to pick up Elizabeth's prescription, then head over to the feed store. I got a lot of working waiting for me when I get back."

The two men shook hands, and Fred turned to go into the drugstore. Jim stayed close behind him, so he could walk through the open door. Oh, he could walk through a closed door—he'd discovered that early on—but he didn't like to. He didn't feel like he should be *able* to.

"Hey there, Mr. Trebble," the girl behind the counter called out. "What can we do you for today?"

Mr. Trebble? Jim about bust out laughing. Mr. Trebble was his daddy, and almost nobody called him that, because he always said, "Let's forget about this Mr. Trebble business; you just call me Harold."

Jim waited for Fred to say the same thing, to say go ahead and call him Fred. But Fred just nodded at the girl and said, "Hey, Prissie, I need to pick up that refill of Elizabeth's prescription."

"She having trouble with her eyes again?"

"'Fraid so. Doctor's still not sure what it is."

Jim wondered if Elizabeth was Fred's wife. If she was, she sounded like a lot of trouble, spending all of his money on dresses and sending him to town to pick up medicine all the time. He wondered what had happened to Mary Lloyd, the girl Fred had taken to the Harvest Dance his junior year. She'd had jet-black hair and blue eyes, and whenever Jim had seen her, his words had gotten all jumbled up in his throat, which made Mary Lloyd laugh in a way he thought sounded nice, almost like singing.

"Your mama doing okay?" the girl asked Fred when she returned from the back of the store with a small paper bag in her hand. "I haven't seen her around much."

"She's middling," Fred told her, taking out his wallet. "It's only been six months, and they were married almost thirty years."

The girl rang up Fred's purchase. "She's had more than her fair share of trials, that's the truth. Your total is two dollars and forty-nine cents."

110

"At least with Daddy we knew it was coming." Fred handed the girl a ten-dollar bill. "Jim—well, he was gone just like that. And then never finding him, just knowing he'd never come back—well—" Fred stopped, swallowed hard, took the bag from the girl.

Jim felt his mind grow hazy, the way it did when he started to think about going down to the river. What was Fred saying about Daddy? He was making it sound like Daddy had—

Jim's mind clouded over.

"Well, I thank you," Fred told the girl, giving her a tip of an imaginary hat. "Tell your daddy I say hey."

Jim tried to follow him out of the store, but he couldn't make his feet go. *Move*, he told himself. *Fred's getting away and you don't know where he's going or how to find him again.* But Jim couldn't move. He couldn't even remember where he was or what he was doing there.

After a minute Jim made his way over to a chair near the door and sat down. Funny, he could almost feel the chair's hard bottom beneath him. Made him think of all those hours sitting at his desk at school, his whole body aching to get outside. Not that he'd hated school. In fact, he wished he were at school right now, copying over his spelling list, the smells from the cafeteria kitchen—sloppy joes and chicken cutlets with gravy—spilling down the hall into Mrs. Porter's classroom and making his stomach growl in anticipation.

He felt a hand on his shoulder, and he twisted around. Daddy?

Ain't your daddy, the boy said. He was small and colored and see-through. Jim knew him. Knew his voice, anyway. He closed his eyes.

You got to come back now, the boy said. He reached down and took Jim's hand. You fading.

Without opening his eyes, Jim said, How'd you find me here?

Followed you. Something told me I better. Now let's go on back. You fading away in here.

Jim nodded and slowly stood. He let the boy lead him toward the door. As they were going out, a woman was coming in, and Jim had a sick feeling as he crossed through her body.

112

"Oh, my goodness, Prissie, I got a chill walking in here!" the woman exclaimed. "I believe somebody just walked over my grave!"

Come on now, the boy said to Jim. I'll get you back to where it's safe.

13

The Drowned Boy

The day after they found the cabin, Wendell woke up and wondered what to do. Go over to George's and get started on plans for a clubhouse? Why didn't that idea excite him more? That was the whole point of finding the cabin in the first place, wasn't it? But now that plan didn't suit him.

Maybe it was George—the notion of George—that was getting in the way. Sure, George was Wendell's best friend, but he had his drawbacks. Living in town the way he did, George could be lazy. He didn't like to travel too far to get to things. Only the week before Wendell had tried to interest him in a trip to Burger World, a five-minute bike ride down Route 16, ten minutes at the most, but George had said, "They've got burgers at Ralph's Grill on Green Street. Why not go there?"

Well, there were plenty of reasons. First of all, Wendell had eaten so many of Ralph's burgers over the years, he thought he might turn into one if he ate any more. Add to that the fact that the fries at Burger World were the best in Celeste, maybe the best ever made. They were fries that were worth a little extra effort. The fact was, food always tasted better if you had to go a mile or two more to get it. You felt like you'd earned it that way.

Wendell rolled out of bed, feeling more irritated with George by the minute. He'd forgotten all about George not wanting to ride out to Burger World, and now he was reliving the whole scene from last week, the two of them sitting at the counter at Ralph's, all the booths filled with teenagers fresh from the swimming pool, their hair still dripping, the smell of chlorine everywhere. It took ten minutes to get their burgers, and then Wendell could hardly eat his, it was so rare. Maybe if the high school kids hadn't of been there, he would have sent it back, but there was no way he was making a fuss in front of them.

Maybe George was the wrong person for this, Wendell thought as he pulled on a pair of jeans. Maybe he needed someone who had a better sense of adventure, someone who wouldn't think twice if you asked him to carry tools and supplies out to the woods. Wendell had been pondering logistics the night before—what they might need to get the cabin into shape. Lumber, for sure, and tools, maybe a ladder. He had a hard time imagining George carrying a ladder farther than ten feet.

He'd hoped he could talk his dad into doing the job with him, but the second Dad walked in the house after work, Wendell knew better than to even bring it up. He had that look on his face, a bad-day look, a *My boss is a pissant and I don't want to talk about it* look. He didn't even eat dinner with them. Instead he took his plate to the porch. The only thing he said to Wendell all night was right before bedtime. Wendell was sitting at his desk, making a list of supplies he'd need to get the cabin in working order, when Dad appeared in the doorway, pointing a finger at him. "No matter what, you ain't ever working in the mill. Don't care how bad you need the money, you ain't working there, not even in the summers when you're in high school. You got that, son?"

Wendell nodded mutely. He hadn't planned on working at the Felts paper mill anyway. From what his dad said, it was too hot, and you did the same thing day in and day out, got to know the number 4 machine—or whatever machine it was you ran—so well that you saw it in your dreams. No, Wendell was planning on playing baseball or owning a car lot when he grew up.

"Good," his dad said, already turning away. "Because if I ever catch you working in the mill, I'll—well, I better not catch you." And then he was off down the hallway, and a few seconds later his bedroom door slammed shut, the sound of it loud as a rifle report.

That's when Wendell got the idea he'd get the cabin fixed up and then show it to his dad. He'd make it a surprise. He was thinking he might save up to get him a new fishing rod, sell the idea of the cabin as a fisherman's hangout. He even went out to the garage and finished whittling two of his new lures and sanded them down, thinking how he'd paint them the same and give one to his dad.

But that was another way George was a problem, Wendell thought now as he made his way downstairs. George didn't care for fishing. He said fish stank and he didn't want to lose an eyeball by getting a hook stuck in it.

Sometimes Wendell wondered how he and George ever got to be friends in the first place.

"If you want eggs, tell me now," his mother called from the kitchen. "I've got just about enough time to scramble some for you, and then I'm off to Miss Bertie's. She needs a ride to the doctor this morning, so I'm going to take her before work."

Wendell's mother was the sort of person

who liked to help out. She and the other women of Grace Baptist Church had a group where they got together and figured out who to help next. Wendell shuddered just to think of it. What if he broke his arm or got hit by a car and got put on their list one day? They'd be coming over and making a big fuss, probably spray a bunch of perfume around his room and fill it up with flowers. No sir, keep the Grace Baptist Church Women's Club away from him.

"I'll just get some cereal," Wendell told his mother, walking into the kitchen. "It's too hot for eggs."

"I know what you mean," his mother said, untying her apron and hanging it on a peg by the pantry door. "I'm thinking I might make a ham mousse for dinner tonight, something nice and cold."

"Is that the one you make with the gelatin?" Wendell asked, his stomach churning a little at the memory. "Where it wiggles on your plate?"

"That's the one!" His mother grabbed her handbag from the counter. "Now, your sisters are babysitting this morning—or I should say

Rosemary is babysitting and Missy's gone with her to help. I'm going to try to leave the office to come home for lunch, but Mr. Bertram says he has a pile of letters to do today, so I may have to spend my lunch hour typing. Leave me a note if you go anywhere. Might be a nice day to go to the new pool."

After his mother left, Wendell poured himself a bowl of cornflakes, flooded it with milk, and stood at the counter to eat his breakfast. Maybe he ought to find Ray Sanders and get him to help out. Ray seemed like the kind of boy who was up for an adventure. He sure got in trouble a lot at school, mostly because he couldn't sit still for more than two minutes. Teachers were always telling him to get back in his seat. "That's all we do in this school," he'd complained once last year to their teacher, Mrs. Appleby. "We just sit at our desks and write stuff down!" Mrs. Appleby had stared at him like she didn't understand what was wrong with that.

Wendell didn't know Ray all that well, but they'd played on the same baseball team last spring, and once after practice they'd ridden their bikes down to Bottomside Creek to cool off. The name Bottomside had made Ray snicker, but it had taken Wendell a second to get the joke, and he felt sort of stupid when he did. Now he'd have to think of people's bottoms every time he went fishing down there.

But that didn't keep him from thinking Ray Sanders was probably all right, and it didn't stop him now from heading over to where Ray lived, which was past Central Street, over where the mill managers had built housing for their workers. Dad wouldn't live there, but then Dad wouldn't live in any place he didn't own. He said he didn't like owing anybody, especially bosses.

Wendell sort of knew where Ray lived, but when he got over to that part of town, he had to ride his bike up and down the streets because all the houses looked alike, red brick with white doors, no shutters, no front porches, just concrete steps. By sheer good luck, Ray's mother was stepping out of a blue Packard just as Wendell was riding past his third time down the street. He knew Mrs. Sanders from baseball games, where she yelled the loudest of all the mothers.

When she saw him, she waved and then turned toward the house and called, "Hey, Ray! Wendell's here!" so loud that Wendell thought every Ray in the neighborhood would come running. A minute later Ray sauntered out of the house, chewing on an apple. When he saw Wendell, he tossed the core into the yard and called, "Wait right there—I'll go get my bike."

For a while they rode around the neighborhood without talking. Ray had playing cards stuck to the spokes of his wheels with clothespins, which made a satisfying clicking noise as he pedaled. Wendell thought he might do that too when he got home, if he could find an old deck of cards. He bet King would like it, the *click-click-click* of it being similar to the sound Wendell made with his tongue against the roof of his mouth when he was calling King in from the yard for dinner.

"Hey, Ray," Wendell said after he'd gotten bored of riding aimlessly, with nothing to look at but the redbrick houses with their white doors and no shutters, one after another on into infinity. "You want to see this place I found yesterday in the woods near the river?"

Ray slowed down, and the clicking sound slowed too. "What'd you find?"

"Just this old cabin," Wendell said with a shrug, playing it down in case Ray thought it was a stupid idea. "My dad and my uncles used to hang out there when they were kids. I was thinking we could turn it into a fisherman's cabin, that sort of thing."

"Might as well," Ray said, sounding less enthusiastic than Wendell would have wished for. "Nothing else to do."

The best way to the river was to ride down through the Bottom and then follow a path through the woods that Ray knew about. The Bottom was where the colored people lived, and Wendell had never spent much time there except to cut through it en route from one place to another. Now as he followed Ray down Marigold Lane, he thought about that girl Callie and wondered where her house was.

He hoped they didn't pass her. She might get suspicious and want to know where they were going. She might guess they were on their way to the cabin and try to stop them, or worse, ask to go with them. Not that she had to ask; it wasn't like the cabin was Wendell's, not really, though he thought that since his dad had been there as a boy, Wendell should have first dibs and get to decide what to do with it.

"This old colored lady might yell at us when we ride through her yard," Ray warned when they reached the place where the pavement puttered out, replaced by dirt and gravel. "Just ignore her."

Wendell thought maybe they ought not ride their bikes across somebody's grass, but he wasn't going to make a federal case out of it. Besides, nobody was around. He could tell, though, from the tomato plants encircled by neat rings of marigolds, that whoever lived here cared about their yard, and so he pedaled faster to get through it quicker.

They had to walk their bikes when they got down to the river. "When we get to the woods, we ought to park them behind some trees," Wendell told Ray. "Ain't no point pushing 'em all the way up."

Bikes stowed away, they headed up the path. Wendell started getting excited as they got closer, but a little scared, too. He'd let himself forget the way that cabin had felt yesterday, how the cold air had wrapped itself around him like it was trying to hold him there. Maybe the cabin had been built over a sinkhole, Wendell thought. Maybe it was cave gas coming up through the ground that made it so cold. He found that a satisfying explanation, aside from the fact that cave gas could kill you if you breathed it too long.

He thought it might be a problem they didn't have King with them to lead the way to the hidden part of the route, but Wendell remembered where it was well enough. "Watch out for poison ivy," he warned Ray as they turned right to go deeper into the woods. "It's everywhere."

"Poison ivy don't bother me none," Ray claimed. "Never has. I'm the only one I know who's that way."

"You're lucky," Wendell told him. "It eats me up alive."

They were closing in on the cabin when Ray gave a low whistle from behind Wendell and whispered, "You hear something?"

Wendell stopped. He heard a squirrel rustling the tree branches and the tapping of a woodpecker off in the distance. He turned to Ray and shook his head.

"I hear talking," Ray told him. "Wish I'd brought my BB gun."

Wendell had to stop himself from laughing out loud. What the heck would a BB gun do in a dangerous situation? Poke a few holes in a person, maybe scare away a groundhog. He was just about to make a smart remark about it when he heard a boy's voice say, "I think you're overthinking this situation, Little Sis."

The voice sounded close and far away at the same time. But that "Little Sis" . . . Shoot! Wendell bet Callie was back and she'd brought someone with her.

"I think I know who it might be," he told Ray in a low voice. "At least, I think I know one of the people who might be there."

"We need to sneak up on 'em?" Ray asked. "Should we ambush 'em?"

Wendell looked at Ray a second. What the heck was he thinking about? "I don't think there's anything to be afraid of."

"I didn't say anything about being afraid," Ray replied, sounding irritated.

They continued toward the cabin, and a minute later they reached the clearing. "Callie? Anybody here?" Wendell called out. As if in response, a dog barked.

He bet the old dog was back. He wondered if he'd ever left.

The sound of footsteps crunched across the undergrowth, and then a tall, skinny colored kid appeared in the clearing. He gave Wendell a long look and said, "You look familiar to me. Why's that?"

"How should I know?" Wendell said, but as soon as he said it, he knew. It was the kid from the drugstore, the one who'd been reading comic books a couple of days ago.

Ray stepped forward. "I think you're the

one who needs to explain yourself. What you doing out here, boy? This ain't your property."

The kid smiled and shrugged. "Ain't your property either, I reckon. Unless you own these woods. I expect you don't."

Wendell stepped between them. "You kin to Callie? Is she out here?"

The boy nodded in the direction of the cabin. "She's over there, trying to make friends with that old dog. Acts like she in love with it."

Wendell could feel Ray behind him, could feel the way he was itching for a fight. "We just came out to take a look at that cabin."

"Us too. Callie wanted me to see it. Wanted me to take a look at that handwriting on the wall."

Wendell had forgotten about that. "What do you think?"

"I think it says 'Jim,' just the way you think."

Wendell heard rustling behind him. When he turned around, Ray was holding a big stick and taking quick steps toward the colored boy.

"I think it's time for you and whoever else you got with you to move on," Ray said, swinging the stick like a batter warming up in the batter's box. "We won't hurt you if you go right now."

"Are you crazy?" Wendell moved so he was blocking Ray from getting any closer to the boy. "Put that down."

"This is our cabin, and this boy here's a trespasser."

Suddenly Wendell was wishing like crazy he'd gone ahead and asked George to come. Sure, George was lazy and he didn't like to fish, but he'd never pull a stunt like this.

The colored kid held up his hand. "Hold up now. Why you swinging that stick? This place don't belong to you. Don't belong to me, either. Far as I know, anybody and everybody's got the right to be here."

"Carl Jr.! Where you at?"

Wendell recognized Callie's voice. *Great*, he thought. *Let's throw a little gasoline on this fire.*

"You stay put, Little Sis," the boy called back. "Just having a neighborly discussion here."

"I ain't your neighbor, Carl Jr.," Ray said, pushing Wendell out of his way as he moved closer. "I'm your worst enemy."

"Cut it out, Ray," Wendell said, his voice shaky. "This is stupid."

"Nothing stupid at all about dealing with trespassers. You got to—"

But Ray didn't have a chance to finish his sentence. Suddenly the old dog was right there, right at Ray's feet, his teeth bared, his growl the kind that let you know he was serious.

"Get your dog away from me," Ray snarled at Carl Jr. "I'll smack it upside the head if you don't."

"Ain't my dog, and I'd like to see you try."

The old dog lunged at Ray, his teeth snapping. "Down!" Ray yelled at him, kicking the dog in the chest and knocking him back a few feet. "Get off of me!"

"Get away from that dog!" Now Callie was there, standing next to her brother. "Get away from him or I'll kill you!"

The dog lunged again, and Ray threw his stick at it. "Come on, Wendell, let's get out of here!" he cried, already running toward the woods. "That dog's crazy!"

"You better get on out of here, both of you!"

Callie yelled. "Or I'm gonna kill you, just like I said."

"Shut up about killing people," Carl Jr. told her. "You ain't killing nobody."

"I'll kill that boy if he runs back this way." She turned and pointed at Wendell. "What you just standing there for? Why ain't you running off with your scaredy-pants friend?"

Wendell felt frozen in place. He held up his hands and shrugged, like, *I don't know what just happened here.*

"Wendell, come on!" Ray's voice called from the path, but Wendell didn't move. If he followed him, then Callie and her brother would think he was like Ray, and it wasn't that Wendell cared all that much what a couple of colored kids thought about him, but he guessed he cared enough. And, dumb as it sounded, he cared what that old dog thought too.

"Go on, then!" Callie said. "This cabin don't belong to you anyway. It's more ours than yours."

That brought Wendell up short. "What do you mean? We were together when we found

131

it. How could it be more yours than mine?"

"I ain't saying. But it's true."

The old dog had trotted over to the start of the path, as if he was interested in whether or not Ray was coming back. Now he came over and stood next to Carl Jr., looking at Wendell with an expression that suggested he didn't much trust him anymore.

Carl Jr. reached down and scratched the old dog's head. "This old place don't belong to nobody except maybe the birds and the squirrels. But maybe you don't agree. Maybe you think like that friend of yours, that me and Callie here are trespassers."

"I don't think that," Wendell said. He almost said he was sorry about Ray, that he didn't know him all that well, and if he'd known he was going to act that way, Wendell wouldn't have brought him here in the first place. But he didn't want to seem like he was kowtowing.

"Maybe you think since you white and Little Sis here's colored, that gives you dibs," Carl Jr. said with a shrug. "She says you keep trying to claim it for your own."

"That's not exactly how I put it," Callie said, sounding sheepish. "Said sometimes he *act* like that's how he think."

Carl Jr. turned to his sister. "So this old Wendell Crow ain't quite so bad as you say? He ain't trying to steal this cabin out from under you?"

Callie leaned down to scratch her knee. "I don't know how bad he is. All I know is I don't like his friends."

"I ain't so crazy about 'em either," Wendell mumbled, and Carl Jr. cracked a grin.

"Yeah, I might trade that stick boy in for a new model," he said. "He got some defects."

Then Carl Jr. gave Wendell a long look, like he was thinking hard about something. "Well, if you ain't the devil in sneakers, then maybe we'll let you in on some things we know. Little Sis has been doing some research."

Callie crossed her arms over her chest. "I ain't telling him nothing."

Carl Jr. popped Callie in the shoulder. "Quit being so muleheaded. You ain't giving away no family secrets here."

"Says you."

Carl Jr. leaned toward his sister and spoke in a low voice. "You don't have to tell him every little thing you know. Just tell him about Jim."

Wendell could tell from Callie's expression that she was dying to spill the beans, she was just too stubborn to do it.

"You find something out about that name on the wall?" he asked, moving a few steps closer. "You figure out who Jim is?"

Callie's arms relaxed just a little bit. "Don't know if there's a connection or not, but I found out something about a boy who drowned."

"Little Sis just felt in her bones the two things were connected, didn't you, girl?"

Pride washed over Callie's face. "Oh, yeah, I been knowing all along everything's tied up together—this here dog and the cabin. Haven't figured everything out yet, but at least I know more than I did."

"So who was the boy that drowned?" Wendell felt a little shaky around the edges, like maybe he'd find out the boy was someone he knew.

"He drowned right down there," Callie said, pointing in the direction of the river. "Went in right at that point at the bottom of the path. They say the water was wild that day, and he got pulled in real fast. They never did find his body, even though folks from all over searched for it from here to Covington."

"You know anything about him—where he lived, what his name was?"

Callie nodded. "I'll tell you what his name was, all right. His name was Jim. And you know what else I know for a fact?"

Wendell shook his head. "What?"

Callie grinned, triumphant. "He had a dog. You're looking at it right now."

14

How Callie Learned
What She Learned

I t had been a strange sight to see Mr. Renfrow
at her front door the evening before. In his
office Mr. Renfrow always seemed relaxed and
easy. But standing on the Robinsons' porch,
he'd had a formal feeling to him. When Callie
got down there, he was speaking with her
mama, and she could see how nervous-making
that was for him.

"Why don't you come in and sit down to
dinner with us, Orin?" her mama was asking as
Callie stepped out onto the porch. "It's not anything fancy—crowder peas with ham and corn

136

bread—but it'll fill you up. You look like you could use yourself a good home-cooked meal."

"I thank you very much, Mrs. Robinson, but I fear the ladies at the Hop would get worried if I didn't come in on chicken-potpie night. Sally makes extra just for me."

Callie's mouth watered at the thought of the chicken potpie at the Hop Diner. The only time they ever got to eat over there was when Mama got one of her headaches and had to go to bed the minute she got home from work. Daddy would give Regina some money, and the three children would walk down to Lexington Street, feeling bad about Mama but good about what was about to go into their bellies.

"Miss Callie!" Mr. Renfrow exclaimed when he saw her, sounding like he was glad to move on from the topic of dinner. "Just the young lady I was looking for!" Then he looked flustered and said, "N-n-not that it hasn't been a delight speaking with you, Mrs. Robinson."

Mama turned to go back inside. "Oh, it's always a pleasure to see you, Orin. I'm going to get you to my dinner table one of these days."

Callie watched Mr. Renfrow watch Mama go back inside, and shook her head. Poor old thing, liking her mama the way he did. "How you doing, Mr. Renfrow? You got some work you need me to do?"

"On the contrary, Miss Callie," Mr. Renfrow replied, regaining his composure. "I hope it's I who can be a help to *you*. You see, after you left today, a memory began dancing around in my mind, dim and distant, about a boy who drowned. It was some time ago, I remembered that much, but I couldn't remember when. And then it came to me—it was the week after the old dry-goods store burned down, the one Mr. Turner owned on Oak Street. You were just a baby then. But it was quite a story because arson was suspected. In fact, some thought that Turner's store had been burnt down so that the colored community would take their business to the new A&P over on Elm Street. Nothing was ever proven, of course. But it was the week after that that a twelve-year-old boy drowned in the Ohio, just down from Jericho's Point, where the river bends. It was in April, right after the spring rains, and the water was running wild. The boy's dog went in after him, and it was thought they both were lost. The boy's body was never found."

"That whole memory came back to you?"

"Oh, no—just the memory of the boy's drowning. But once I remembered that it was after Turner's store burned down, it was easy enough to find the story in the following week's paper. I thought you might like to read it."

"Oh, I'm interested," Callie said. "Definitely interested."

Mr. Renfrow pulled a yellowed, folded-up paper from a large pocket inside his jacket. "You may keep this copy. There are follow-up stories for several weeks, if you'd like to come down to the office to read them."

Callie took the paper and unfolded it. It was dated April 16, 1943. The story above the fold was about colored soldiers from Celeste who were fighting the war in Germany. Underneath that story was the headline CELESTE BOY LOST IN OHIO RIVER; PRESUMED DEAD and below the headline were two pictures. One was a school

139

picture of a regular-looking white boy, brownish hair, light eyes, sticking-out teeth. The other one was of the old dog, only he wasn't old in the picture. He looked downright youthful.

"That's the old dog!" she told Mr. Renfrow, pointing at the picture. "The old dog belonged to that drowned boy. Only if that's the old dog, well, he didn't drown like folks thought."

"No, he didn't," Mr. Renfrow agreed. "Not if that's him. Perhaps you should write a story for the paper about it. Everyone likes a good dog story."

Callie nodded, wishing like anything dogs could talk. Where'd that old dog been all these years? That would be the real story right there.

"And I thought perhaps you could write something about the boy. Go talk to his family, ask for some background information, paint a fuller picture. Rereading this story, I see there's not much about the boy at all, except his name and age."

His name? Callie scanned the cutline under the pictures: "Jim Trebble."

The boy's name was Jim.

So Jim wasn't some old guy living in a shack by the river. He was a boy, and maybe that made more sense. A boy was more likely to carve his name in a wall than a man, she reckoned. What had he been doing up in the cabin, though?

"I believe the boy's father recently passed," Mr. Renfrow informed her. "But his mother still lives on West Main. She might enjoy reminiscing about her son."

After dinner Callie took the paper upstairs to her room, sat down on her bed, and studied on it. Turned out this Jim Trebble had been fishing down at the river with two friends when a big wind came up and blew his hat off into the water. "That was Jim's lucky hat," one of his friends, a boy named Robert Lincoln, was quoted as saying. "Only I guess it wasn't so lucky that day."

I guess not, Callie thought, and read on. Jim Trebble had gone out into the water to retrieve his hat, which was racing away toward where the river deepened. His friends reported that just as he was about to reach the hat, he slipped, went under, and didn't come back up.

Didn't come back up. Callie shivered. Imagine that. She'd been pulled under the water a time or two herself, and even though it had only been for a few seconds each time, she'd never forgotten what it felt like to go tumbling over the rocks, the river pulling at you like it had some place it needed you to be. Both times Daddy had snatched her up out of the water and carried her back to the banks, fussing at her about being more careful. Now she guessed she could see his point. Looked like the river could carry you all the way away if it felt like it.

Callie leaned back against her pillow and stared at the picture of Jim Trebble. According to the article, he'd been in sixth grade at the old elementary school on East Main Street, the one all the white kids went to before they built Thomas Edison Elementary a few blocks up. Now the old elementary school was a community center.

Mr. Renfrow was right. The article didn't say a whole lot about Jim Trebble as a person, only that he'd had a dog called Buddy, and Buddy had jumped into the river to save him, had yet to be found, and was presumed drowned along with his owner. *Shows you how much they knew*, Callie thought. *That old dog's tough like me. Takes more than an old river to bring us down.*

"Whatcha looking at, Little Sis?" Carl Jr. was standing in the doorway. He must have sniffed out the fact that Callie was onto something interesting. "Why'd Mr. Renfrow bring you that paper?"

"I told y'all at dinner, that's between me and Mr. Renfrow. You'll find out when it's time."

Carl Jr. walked over and sat down next to Callie on her bed. "Maybe I could help you out, whatever it is you're doing. I ain't got nothing else on my docket at this very minute."

"Where's Everett at?" Everett was Carl Jr.'s best friend, and usually after supper the two of them would be outside hitting a ball around or getting into mischief.

"Gone to Cincinnati to see his granny. Won't be back till next week."

"So you're bored and want to stick your nose into my business."

Carl Jr. looked at Callie and shook his head.

"Just trying to be of service, Little Sis. You don't got to get all high and mighty on me."

Callie folded up the paper and put it behind her pillow. She needed to think about this for a minute. On the one hand, she didn't want Carl Jr. to butt in on her project. He might get the notion all of a sudden that he was a newspaper reporter and decide to take over her investigation into the life of Jim Trebble and the old dog.

On the other hand, she wouldn't mind having someone to go back to the cabin with her. That old Wendell Crow didn't count. First of all, she didn't know how to find him, and second of all, she didn't trust him. She'd only known him for two days! *White boys like trouble*, wasn't Mama always saying that?

Still, the fact was Callie didn't want to go back to the cabin by herself. That place felt funny. Felt cold and, well, *occupied*. Wendell had pretended like he hadn't noticed it, but Callie could tell he was feeling something strange too, the way he kept rubbing his arms and looking all around, like there was a snake in there or something.

144

And the way Wendell's dog, King, wouldn't come inside? What made him stop at the door?

No, Callie didn't cherish the thought of going back there by herself.

"Okay," she finally said to Carl Jr. "I'm gonna tell you, but you keep in mind that I'm the boss of this."

Carl Jr. grinned. "Whatever you say, Little Sis."

The next day she and Carl Jr. had walked to the cabin, even though Carl Jr. thought Callie was nuts. "You know there ain't no ghosts, don't you?"

"No, I don't know that. You're gonna feel what I'm talking about when we get there, just you wait. And I bet that old dog's still sitting there too. Now, why do you think that is?"

"Maybe that's where he stay. Everybody needs a home, even an old dog."

"Maybe," Callie said, just to end the argument for a minute. She was starting to feel nervous the closer they got to the cabin. Now that she knew for sure that the old dog had belonged to the boy who drowned, she couldn't stop thinking about that name scrawled on the wall. She just knew it had to be the same Jim as the Jim Trebble she'd read about in the newspaper.

"Might be the same," Carl Jr. agreed after they'd reached the cabin and she'd pointed out the name on the wall to him. "Might not be, though. Probably a million Jims live around here."

"Jim Trebble lived over on the edge of town, is what the paper says, on West Main Street."

"So he could've been here. All sorts of folks been in this cabin over the years."

Callie put her hand on her brother's arm and squeezed it. Hard. "I think this is where the runaway slaves hid," she whispered, her voice trembling with the excitement of it. "You know, like Mama Lou told us about?" This was the first time Callie had said it out loud.

"Could be," Carl Jr. agreed. He looked around the cabin. "Hard to think that they wouldn't have got caught easy if dogs got hold of their scent. Maybe there used to be something to hide inside of."

They'd been looking around the outside of the cabin, the old dog trailing them, when they heard someone calling, "Callie? Anybody here?" from the clearing. Had to be Wendell.

"You stay here," Carl Jr. told her. "Let me check this out."

"But you don't even know him, and I do," Callie argued. "That don't make sense."

"You just stay here." The tone of his voice let her know he was serious, and Carl Jr. didn't get serious about much, so Callie stayed put.

Once the old dog got to barking, though, she just had to go and see what the matter was. And there was Wendell Crow, looking nervous and confused, and that boy behind him, red faced and squinty eyed, waving a stick around!

Well, that sure proved one thing, didn't it? Callie had been right not to trust that old Wendell. Bringing boys with sticks up to her cabin! After Stick Boy ran off, Wendell just stood there, not even bothering to explain himself. Wasn't he something, acting stuck up that way?

But she could tell he was interested when she said she knew something about that name on the wall. And his eyes nearly popped out of his head when she said that the old yellow dog had belonged to a boy named Jim who drowned in the river.

"But you don't know it's the same Jim that wrote his name in the cabin," Wendell said. "I can think of at least four Jims who live around here right off the top of my head. I go to school with Jim Laughlin and Jim Lange, and they don't live but a mile or two down the road."

Carl Jr. nodded. "I know a lot of Jims too. But Callie here thinks there's only one Jim who ever lived in Celeste, and it just so happens he likes to sign his autograph."

Callie stuck her hands on her hips and was about to say something sharp as a serpent's tooth to Carl Jr., but nothing came to mind, so she stomped off back to the cabin. *Wish this old place had the kind of door you could slam*, she thought as she stepped across the cabin's threshold. It would be mighty satisfying to slam a door right now.

"Aw, come on, Little Sis," Carl Jr. called from the clearing. "I'm only joking around!"

Callie ignored him. She circled around the

inside of the cabin, looking up and down. Had to admit Carl Jr. was right about one thing—how could anybody have hidden in a place like this? If dogs had come to the door, that would have been that, the runaways would have been caught in a thin second. She looked over at the wooden bed frame. Could somebody have hidden by hanging on to those ropes underneath a mattress or a quilt?

She walked over to the bed. It was awful small for hiding under. Bending down, Callie examined the underneath and figured a dog could find you there as well as out in the open. Still, she slid herself under, just to get a feel for it. She turned so she was lying on her back and stared up at the frayed ropes, imagined herself hanging on to them, pulling herself up as close to the frame as she could. No, she just couldn't see how that would make for a good hiding place. First of all, unless you were some kinda muscleman, you wouldn't be able to hang there for more than ten seconds.

Callie lay there for a minute, pondering. Brushing away some dirt from beside her on the floor, she felt something, a little hole just the right size to fit her finger into. Callie bet the floor was as holey as Swiss cheese, as bad a shape as this place was in. She felt around some more, but no, it was just that one hole. Callie flipped back over and examined it, poking her finger deeper in, hoping like anything there weren't no snakes or rats hungry for a tasty girl's fingertip, but all she could feel was the air. As she pulled her finger back out, the floor gave a little. Callie hooked her finger into a C and pulled hard. The floor beneath her knees groaned softly, like all that was holding it down was the weight of her.

Callie slid out from underneath the bed frame and pulled it away from the wall. The cabin was dark, but kneeling again, she could just about see the shape of a square cut into the floor. Standing so that she was on the outside of the square, she leaned over and stuck her finger back into the hole. Sure enough, the square lifted up. It was a trapdoor!

Carefully, Callie pulled the door all the way up and over, so it was lying flat on the floor. Peering down into the hole, she couldn't see anything, so she figured there was only one thing to do: go down inside it herself.

Callie leaned back on her heels. Problem was, it was awful dark down there. Might be some sort of critters hiding out, a big old raccoon or some rats. Callie wasn't afraid of nothing, she just liked to see what she was heading into. Hard to warm up to the idea of sticking her foot down blind and having something nibble on her ankle.

Well, what was her plan, then? Wait for Wendell Crow to come and plant a flag down there? All he cared about was who got dibs on the cabin. If he found this hiding place, why, he'd say it was for putting down crates of pop or storing his fishing tackle. *I went down first*, he'd say, *so it's all mine.*

"Callie, where'd you go?" Carl Jr. called out from outside the cabin. Callie slipped down into the darkness. Nothing tried to bite or grab her, so maybe she'd scared away anything that called this place home. The space wasn't deep, and it was easy to lean over and pull the trapdoor back down over her head. She was careful to do it slow, bending down as she did. There was just enough room for her to squat. She wished she had a light so she could see how big the space was and see what else was down here, but once the door was back down, there was only a tiny bit of light coming through that tiny hole, and Callie could hardly see a thing.

Feeling around with her hands, Callie checked to make sure there wasn't anything on the ground to bite her or get up her britches, and when it seemed like there wasn't, she sat down on her bottom. The trapdoor was just a foot or so over her head.

"Callie? Come on now, girl! Show yourself!"

Callie grinned. Now she knew where the slaves had hidden, and Carl Jr. didn't have the least little idea. Man alive, she was good at solving mysteries. Might be she'd grow up to be a private investigator someday. She guessed she could be a reporter, too, like Mr. Renfrow, since he was always looking into stuff, like who robbed the Laundromat that one time or whatever happened to Mrs. Anderson's cat that disappeared, but she thought maybe a private investigator wouldn't have to follow all the rules the way Mr. Renfrow had to. A private investigator might could skirt the law a little in order to get to the bottom of things.

Even when her eyes adjusted, Callie couldn't see much more than the back of her hand. But after a minute or two she could feel something sort of cold and shapeless pressing against her. She waved her hand around in the air, but there wasn't a thing there.

"Anybody in here?" she asked the air, hoping like anything nothing would answer her back.

"Callie, is that you?" Carl Jr.'s voice came from inside the cabin. "Where the heck are you?"

Callie thought about not answering, but that cold feeling kept pressing against her, and she didn't know how much longer she was going to be able to tolerate it. She got back in a kneeling position, put her hands on the board above her head, and pushed hard.

The board didn't budge an inch. Callie tried three more times, but still no luck. And now when Carl Jr. called out "Callie!" it sounded like his voice had gotten farther away, like he'd given up looking for her in the cabin.

"Carl Jr.!" she cried out. "I'm down here! Help me!" She pushed at the trapdoor again, harder this time. Was she going to be stuck down here forever? What if there was something down here, snakes or rats or something even worse? Panic rose in Callie's throat, and she tried to yell again, but no sound came out of her.

Then the trapdoor opened with a creaky groan, and Wendell's face was peering down inside the hole. He reached out a hand. "You need some help out of there?"

Callie almost said no. Wendell Crow was the last person in the world she wanted help from. But then that cold feeling pressed against her again, and she put her hand in Wendell's. "You better not be laughing," she said.

"I ain't laughing." And he wasn't lying; his mouth was set straight as a pencil. He leaned back his weight, and Callie popped out of the hole.

"So what's down there?" Wendell asked. "You reckon that's where the people who lived here stored their food?"

"I reckon that's where they stored something," Callie told him, which was all she was telling him. She brushed off the back of her skirt, wiped some dirt off of her knees. Seeing his face close up brought her angry feelings back up to the surface.

"What were you thinking about, bringing that boy here? You know he was gonna pull a stick on us?"

"No, I didn't. I wish he hadn't."

From the look on Wendell's face, Callie could tell it cost him something to say that. Not that she cared. "Well, you better not bring him back again."

"Don't think he'll want to come back. He wasn't all that interested to begin with."

"He sure got interested when he found out there was somebody up here to beat with a stick."

Wendell turned and walked over to the fireplace. "You really think that boy that drowned knew about this place?" He was looking at where the name Jim was carved in the wall.

"I know of one way to find out," Callie said, the idea coming to her right then. She'd been worrying the whole day about how she was going to walk up to Jim Trebble's house and ask his mama to talk to her about her drowned son. Who was she to Jim Trebble's mama? Just some eleven-year-old colored girl who'd never known her boy to begin with. Mrs. Trebble would probably shoo her away, and then she'd have to go back to Mr. Renfrow empty handed.

"Oh, yeah, how's that?" Wendell asked, his finger tracing the air over the carved-out name.

"You and me are gonna go talk to his mama. And we're taking that old dog with us."

15

The Weekly Advance

O rin Renfrow arrived at work Friday morning at seven fifteen. He always came in early on the day the paper was published in order to take care of any pressing business before the real work of the day began. At approximately eight thirty, five stacks of newspapers, each one bound with twine, exactly 246 papers in all, would be tossed off the back of a Hatcher's Printing Company truck onto the sidewalk in front of the *Weekly Advance* office. Mr. Renfrow would be standing at the door, waiting for them.

Seven fifteen was especially early for Mr. Renfrow to come in, but today was a special day. His editorial about the need to integrate the town pool was in today's paper, and he was expecting an especially vociferous response. Many of his readers would be against the idea. *Don't trouble the water,* they'd write in impassioned letters to the editor. *Leave well enough alone.* He'd be stopped on the street, interrupted while eating his meat-and-three at the Hop, called up in the middle of the night. *Let's just keep the peace around these parts.* Marcus Overby, who'd moved up to Celeste from Greenville, Mississippi, would take him aside after church on Sunday and say, *You don't understand how bad things can get when you start messing with white folks. We got it good here, Orin. We live our lives, they live theirs. Believe me—that's the way you want it to be.*

Mr. Renfrow understood. Why rock the boat? White folks and black folks had always gotten along well enough in Celeste, mostly by staying out of each other's way. White folks were happy to take colored money; they'd even let you walk through the front doors of their restaurants to pick up your food instead of making you come around through a back alley to get it through the kitchen window. White and colored worked together at the paper mill, and though no colored worker ever got advanced through the line up to management, from what he'd heard and observed, the mill was a good place for a colored man to work. The bosses didn't seem to care what hue your skin was if you did the job you were told to do.

There was an uneasy peace between white and colored in Celeste, and Mr. Renfrow understood how fragile it was, and how scared colored folks were about breaking it. He himself had a cousin in Breckinridge County who'd been lynched twenty years before, dragged from the county jail after he'd been accused of attacking a white woman. Violence was never far from the surface of any human relations. Folks were right to fear it.

Even so, he couldn't help but believe that the world was changing. Colored men had fought alongside white troops on the battlefields of

Europe during World War II, and only the year before, a federal court had heard a brilliant young Negro lawyer argue that the schools of America should be open to all. There were rumblings all around. Mr. Renfrow read colored newspapers from across the country—the *Chicago Defender*, the *Carolina Times*, the *Tri-State Defender*, the *Jackson Advocate*—and there was no doubt in his mind that a new day was on its way. He felt his editorial was a small but necessary step toward bringing that day closer.

So after he'd taken care of the daily business of the *Advance*, he made his way to the sidewalk in front of the office and waited for the truck's arrival. Although it was early, the day was already promising to be hot, and Mr. Renfrow wished he had thought to bring a fresh shirt with him that morning. He planned to deliver the mayor's copy of the paper to him in person. Every mayor of Celeste received a complimentary subscription, but Mr. Renfrow was not convinced that any of them had ever read it. Perhaps Mayor Fowley would feel more inclined to read the *Weekly Advance* if its editor was standing directly across his desk from him.

A truck rumbled up Lexington Street, and Mr. Renfrow readied himself. As soon as the papers landed on the pavement, the work would be continuous until the last one was delivered to its reader. At nine Marvin Booker and Sheldon Keyes, his paper carriers, would arrive to begin folding papers and stuffing them into canvas bags, and by eleven fifteen they would begin delivery. The minute they left the office, Mr. Renfrow would pick up a grilled cheese sandwich at the Hop and be back at his desk by eleven forty-five, ready for the phone to begin ringing. At one o'clock, he would take the paper to the mayor, folded open to his editorial.

"Morning, Orin!" the driver, a young white man by the name of Mac Anderson, called out, and Mr. Renfrow tried not to bristle. He was a good forty years older than Mac; did he not deserve the respect of an honorific? Well, he supposed that was a fight for another day.

"Good morning, Mac. I trust you're well."

"Fine and dandy. I've only got two more

deliveries this morning, and then the rest of the day I'll be working inside, get out of this heat."

"That's fine, just fine. Let me get the front door propped open, and we can begin."

Mr. Renfrow loved the sight of the neat stacks of the *Weekly Advance* sitting in the back of the Hatcher's Printing Company truck. Each copy was a collection of his week's work. Oh, some weeks there was little news to report— a church supper, a dry city council meeting— and he didn't feel as though he'd accomplished much. But even at the end of a slow week the phone still started ringing thirty minutes after the papers had gone out for delivery—praise for a good recipe on the women's page, a question about a council ruling, a comment about his weekly editorial. Even on slow weeks Mr. Renfrow felt he was performing a service to his community.

"You want help carrying those papers in?" Mac asked from his perch on the truck's back bumper. "I got a little extra time."

"No, thank you, son," Mr. Renfrow replied, watching Mac's face to see if it registered annoyance at being called "son" by a colored man. But Mac's countenance remained open and cheerful. Maybe if Mr. Renfrow had been younger, Mac would have taken offense. *The older you get, the more harmless they think you are*, he thought as he lifted the first bundle, staggering a bit under its weight.

By the time he'd carried in the fifth bundle, he knew he would have to go home and change shirts. The temperature had risen sharply in just the last twenty minutes, and the shirt he had on was already damp. When he sighted Marvin riding toward him on his bike, he called that he had an errand to run and would return shortly. Marvin had been working for him for three summers now and could be trusted to get down to work without Mr. Renfrow's supervision.

At nine in the morning the stores and shops along Lexington Street were just beginning to come alive, the exception being the Laundromat, which opened at six thirty every morning and had already been doing a brisk business by the time Mr. Renfrow passed by.

Shirley Markham was standing in front of Shirley's Grocery fussing with her keys, and Mr. Renfrow tipped his hat to her. Shirley had opened her store two years after Turner's Dry Goods burned down, giving folks from the Bottom a place to go for milk and bread if they didn't want to do a big shop at the A&P over on Elm, which was a good twenty-minute walk for those who didn't have cars.

Mr. Renfrow's small house was on River Street, and it was as he was walking down Marigold and just about to turn right onto Calvin to cross over to River that he spotted young Callie Robinson coming up Marigold toward him. She had the old yellow dog on a leash, and walking beside her was a white boy Mr. Renfrow had never seen before.

"Hello, Miss Callie," he called, speeding his steps. He forgot all about the need to get a new shirt, his desire for neatness no match for his desire for a good story. "What has you out on this fine morning?"

"I'm going to see Jim Trebble's mama, just like you said. Old Wendell here's coming with me, since he's the one who helped me find Jim's dog."

Mr. Renfrow raised an eyebrow but didn't say what he was thinking. He knew Callie Robinson well enough to know that she wasn't one to share glory. She was taking that white boy for protection or to appear more legitimate.

"I see. Does she know that you're coming?"

"Nah, I thought it'd be better to surprise her. If she knew we were coming, she might run out the back door."

Mr. Renfrow turned to the boy. "I don't believe I've made your acquaintance, young man. What is your name?"

The boy shoved his hands in his pockets. "Wendell," he mumbled, barely audible. "Wendell Crow."

"And why are you on this errand with Miss Callie, Wendell Crow?"

"I dunno," the boy said, shrugging. "She asked me to go."

"Are the two of you friends?"

"Wouldn't say that, exactly. We just sort of know each other."

Mr. Renfrow nodded. "Interesting. Well, I'm Orin Renfrow, editor of the *Weekly Advance*. Are you familiar with it?"

The boy shook his head no, and Mr. Renfrow held back a sigh of annoyance. "Do you read any newspaper? Do your parents subscribe to the *Covington News* or the *Lexington Herald*?"

More shaking of the head. Well, then, Mr. Renfrow wouldn't take the boy's lack of interest in the *Advance* personally. "If you're ever interested in taking a look around a newspaper office, please stop by. We're over on Lexington Street. Perhaps the two of you could come by this afternoon, after your visit with Mrs. Trebble."

"It's my story, Mr. Renfrow," Callie reminded him. "Don't you go trying to steal it."

"I wouldn't think of it, Miss Callie. But I can't help but be interested in what Mrs. Trebble has to say." Mr. Renfrow leaned over and scratched the old dog behind the ears. "Does she even know, for instance, that Buddy here is alive and well?"

"I wondered about that too," Callie replied.

"I've seen him by the river and around the Bottom, but I don't know where else he goes. Nowadays if you want to find him—" Callie stopped abruptly, covering her mouth with her hand to stop the rest of her sentence from coming out.

"If you want to find him?" Mr. Renfrow asked leadingly. "Is there somewhere he stays now?"

"Bend of the river," Callie said, flashing a look at Wendell. "He almost always stays there now."

"Mmm-hmm," Mr. Renfrow replied, surprised that Callie was such a bad liar. Must not have had enough practice. He looked at his watch and frowned. Nine fifteen. The morning was getting away from him. But he was intrigued by this startling duo standing in front of him. From the expression on Wendell Crow's face, he'd venture that the boy was here under some duress, perhaps against his own will. Nonetheless, something interesting was going on.

He'd picked the right time to pen his

swimming pool editorial, Mr. Renfrow decided as he waved good-bye to Callie and Wendell and hurried toward his house. Because a black girl and a white boy walking a dog down the street together was not something you saw every day.

In fact, Mr. Renfrow had never seen it before in his life.

16

The Road Home Is Through the Window

Jim and Thomas had been sitting quietly in the cabin, Jim on the rickety chair under the window, Thomas on the edge of the bed frame, when the racket outside started. "Buddy, where are you, boy?" the colored girl's voice called out, and Buddy gave a welcoming bark from the yard. For some reason he didn't like to come inside. Maybe he felt like he needed to stand guard, Jim thought.

They's folks here all the time now, Thomas said from the bed. Folks and dogs. Don't like them dogs, though. I know that yellow one yours, and I expect he all right. But that other one? That King? I don't know about him.

Jim turned and looked at Thomas. So tell me again what happened yesterday?

How many times I got to say it? Yesterday that girl come down in the hole there with me. Wasn't but ten minutes after you went off chasing after your shadow again. Callie's what they called her. I tried to talk to her, but she kept slapping at me, like she don't want me around.

Jim smiled to himself. He'd had that same feeling about Thomas about a hundred times. He wondered if Callie had a little brother or sister, somebody who pestered her all the daylong. Or was she the youngest, like him? He knew Wendell had sisters, so he'd know what it was like to want somebody out of your hair. Only Jim was getting used to Thomas now. Was glad for his company.

The voices grew louder. "Buddy! Come here, boy!"

Jim had been feeling better about things now that Buddy was here. *All you need is one good dog*, his daddy used to say. *A dog'll stick by you when other folks won't.* That sure was true of Buddy, who had slept at the end of Jim's bed every night and walked him all the way to school in the morning. He was waiting at the school door at the end of the day too.

Where had Buddy been before that day he showed up at the cabin with Wendell and that girl Callie? And why did he look so old? Fred, too. Strange seeing his big brother look like a man.

Jim leaned back in his chair and tried to do his remembering exercises, but his mind fought hard against him. What had happened to him? When had it happened? He kept seeing a picture of his friends Robert Lincoln and Harry Partin standing on his front porch, fishing poles in hand, and he could remember setting off down the road with them, Buddy trotting along behind them. Must have been headed to the river with all that gear, but Jim couldn't picture ever getting there. Right there was where his memory stopped.

"Buddy, come here!"

Jim stood next to the door, wondering if

someone would push it open so he wouldn't have to walk through. He wished he could put a sign on the door that said DON'T SHUT DOOR! Wished he could let people know what the rules were.

Go through the window if you don't want to go through the door, Thomas said, and Jim whipped around to look at him. How'd he know that's what Jim had been thinking?

Window's wide open, Thomas said.

How—how do *you* go out?

Don't bother me none to walk through a closed door. But I reckon you don't like it much, way you always waiting around like you hoping God push it open for you.

It makes my stomach hurt to walk through walls, Jim admitted.

You get over that after a while.

But Jim didn't want to get over it. Getting over it would mean accepting something he didn't want to accept. If you got used to walking through walls, it meant you were the type of person who *could* walk through walls. Jim wanted to be the type of person who *couldn't* walk through a wall. The type of person who cast a shadow when the sun shone behind him and whose voice made a sound when he opened his mouth to speak.

Go through the window. He guessed that was good advice, so he turned, stepped on the rickety chair, and pulled himself through the opening. He knew he didn't have to do that, that he could have floated up and out, but no. That's not how he did things. Not how he *wanted* to do things.

"That's a good boy," somebody was saying, and when Jim turned the corner, he saw Callie snapping a collar on Buddy's neck, Buddy wriggling this way and that to get out of her grasp. What was she doing, taking his dog? Was she taking him to the vet? *Good luck, Callie,* Jim wanted to tell her. But what if she had other ideas? She looked like a girl who had the good sense to want a dog like Buddy for her own.

Come here, boy, Jim called in his windy voice. Buddy's ears lifted, but he didn't come. Instead he struggled as Callie tried to hook a

173

leash to the collar. Behind her stood Wendell, looking uncomfortable.

"I knew he'd be here this morning," Callie said, finally getting the leash hooked on. "I think this is where he's staying all the time now. He looks skinny, too, like he's not getting anything to eat."

"I'll bring him some food this afternoon," Wendell said, and Jim wished he could say thanks so that Wendell could hear him. He hated to think of Buddy going hungry, but he hadn't figured out a way to feed him.

"Maybe he'll go live with Jim's mama after we bring him over," Callie said. "Maybe he'll be happy to stay there."

"Don't you think that he'd be staying with them already if that's what he wanted?"

"Don't know. Maybe."

Jim felt a wind rush through him. Wendell and this girl were taking Buddy to his house? Why hadn't Buddy been living there? Where had Buddy been?

Where had Jim been?

Buddy! he called again, and this time Buddy

looked in his direction and sniffed the air.

The girl stood and tugged at Buddy's leash. "Come on, boy. We're gonna go see Jim Trebble's mama."

You gonna go with 'em? Thomas was standing next to Jim, his back pressed against the cabin wall, as though he was trying to stay as far away from Buddy as possible.

I reckon, Jim said. I'd like to see my mama. I keep hoping to run into her, but I never do.

How 'bout your daddy? You want to see him, too?

I think my daddy—well, I think he's—

But Jim couldn't say what he thought his daddy was.

Thomas took a tentative step away from the cabin. I best be going with you, he told Jim. You start fading like you did yesterday, that might be the end of you. Then who I'm gonna talk to?

Jim nodded. He was starting to think it was nice to have someone to talk to. He'd almost forgotten what that was like.

17

When Jim Trebble's Mama Opened the Door

Wendell was starting to wish his dad had never brought up the cabin in the woods in the first place. If he hadn't, then Wendell wouldn't be walking through town with a colored girl, feeling stupid and out of sorts. He had pretty much gone unnoticed his entire life, and he'd liked it that way. Every once in a while he made a standout catch in left field or earned the only A on a math test, and it was fine to get the two minutes of attention either of those things were worth. But as a rule Wendell liked to go about his day without anyone giving him much thought.

Walking through the Bottom with Callie Robinson and Buddy? Wendell felt like the whole world was looking at him. One man even stopped his truck in the middle of the street, rolled down his window, and stuck his head out, just to get a better view of their circus act. They'd seen white people down here before, hadn't they? There was even one white family, the Arnettes, who lived in the Bottom. Stanley Arnette was known for saying he thought colored folks were more neighborly than whites. He was also known for being halfway crazy, though Wendell's mother said that wasn't true, it was just that the Arnettes had always been a little bit different from other people.

Wendell didn't have any interest at all in being different. He had absolutely zero interest in walking up Marigold Lane with Callie Robinson, but for some reason he felt like he had to. That stupid Ray Sanders and his stick!

Wendell couldn't help but feel bad about that. He couldn't help feeling like now he owed Callie something.

You just don't like a dog being mad at you, Wendell thought, and that was true enough. In fact, he was pretty sure half the reason he was doing this was because of the way Buddy had looked at him after Ray Sanders ran off into the woods. Wendell could live with a lot of things, but he couldn't live with the idea that a dog like Buddy thought poorly of him.

"We turn left up there," Callie said, pointing toward Main Street. "And then I figure it's about a five-minute walk. Mr. Renfrow says Mrs. Trebble's house is right at the edge of town, where things start turning back into countryside."

That was going to be the hard part—turning right onto Main. Main Street was a street, but it was also a line you crossed to get from the colored part of town to the white part of town. It was bad enough being seen walking with Callie in the Bottom; what about when white folks saw them together?

Wendell looked at Buddy and wondered for the thousandth time in his life what it was like to be a dog. Buddy didn't care who was what— if you were colored or white or a boy or girl. He just kept going along his way, looking for whatever it was he was looking for.

"Come this way, Buddy," Callie instructed the dog when they reached Main Street, tugging him toward the left. "We're going to your old house. Then we're going to write a newspaper article about you."

"I ain't writing any article," Wendell said. "I don't even like to write."

"I didn't mean you. Mainly I just meant me."

"Then why'd you say 'we'?"

Callie stopped and looked at him. "You always so touchy?"

"I ain't touchy."

"Oh, you're touchy, all right. You scared to be seen with a colored girl?"

"Scared to be seen with a crazy girl, is more like it."

Callie tugged at Buddy's leash again and started walking. "You think I'm stupid or something? Don't think I don't know what you're thinking. Thinking how bad it be if some of your friends see us walking down the street. Like I'm giving you cooties or something."

"How do I know you won't?"

"'Cause I'm colored?"

"Because you're a girl."

Callie grinned. "I bet I'm cleaner than you. You ought to check behind your ears, Wendell Crow. A man could start a farm back there."

Wendell felt a laugh coming up, but he managed to turn it into a snort at the last second. "The backs of my ears ain't none of your business."

"Well, thank the Lord for tender mercies."

Wendell shook his head. Girls.

They walked in silence for a few blocks, the sound of birds yakking in the trees filling in the empty space where their conversation had been. To Wendell's relief, there wasn't much traffic and he didn't see many people out in their yards. The few he did see didn't seem to take much notice of their little gang. Maybe he was making too much of a big deal out of it.

This couldn't be the first time in human history a boy had walked down the street with a colored girl and a dog. Probably happened two or three times a year at least. Just because Wendell had never witnessed such a thing himself didn't mean it couldn't be.

"I bet that's it there." Callie was pointing at a house up the street, but Wendell was looking at Buddy, whose tail and ears were sticking up at full attention. Buddy seemed to know exactly where he was without having to read a street number or know the address.

Maybe seeing what happened when Jim Trebble's mama opened the front door and saw Buddy would be worth the embarrassment of walking down the street with a colored girl, Wendell thought. Or at least halfway worth it.

The Trebbles' house was the last one on the right. It was different from the other houses on the street. Set far back off the road, it was standing in a field, its gravel drive cutting a swathe through a blanket of wildflowers.

"It sure turned into country quick out here,"

Callie said, turning to look at the street behind them. "It's like a regular street running through town, and all the sudden—bam! Welcome to nature."

Wendell nodded. That was what it was like, all right. He wondered if Mrs. Trebble lived here all by herself. It gave him a sad feeling to think that she did, the house being set apart from the others the way it was. Well, just about everything concerning the Trebble family made him feel sad. Their boy drowning in the river that way—Wendell winced to think of it. How many times had he been swimming right where Jim Trebble went in? Maybe a million. And he'd been pulled under a time or two, no doubt about it. He knew what that felt like.

"Okay, so here's the plan," Callie began as they started up the gravel drive. "I'll stand a few feet back while you knock on the door. You tell her that you're working over at the *Celeste Gazette and Informer* for the summer, kind of like a volunteer, and you been tracking down the story about Buddy here. Tell her that Buddy's

182

been staying at my house, and that's why I'm here with you."

"But you're the one writing the story."

"Yeah, but that don't matter. It'll make more sense to her that you're the one writing it."

Wendell guessed he could see Callie's point. He didn't know how he felt about lying to Mrs. Trebble, though. Seemed like her life had been hard enough without some kid she didn't even know standing on her front porch telling her lies.

His heart started beating a mile a minute the second he knocked on the front door, and he could feel his palms getting all sweaty. Buddy was standing right at his heels. What if seeing Jim's old dog gave Mrs. Trebble a heart attack? Wendell hadn't even thought about that. *Oh, Lord*, he prayed, *please let her not be home*.

A pair of eyes appeared at the window, and a moment later the door opened to reveal a woman still in her bathrobe. She had a pleasant if somewhat confused expression on her face. "Well, goodness, I wasn't expecting company so early. Is there something I can help you all with?"

Wendell opened his mouth, but the words froze up in his throat. What was it that Callie had told him to say?

"Well, hello there, uh, ma'am," he finally croaked. "I'm writing a report for school and I—"

"For school? In the middle of July?"

"No, not for school, that's not what I meant. What I meant was . . . that is, what I meant to say—"

"He's writing for the newspaper, ma'am," came Callie's voice behind him. "That's what he means. He's volunteering over there this summer, the way some young people do. You know, for career experience?"

The woman nodded, but looked unsure. "For career experience? But the both of you look a little young to be thinking about careers."

"You see, it's like this, ma'am," Callie said, pushing her way past Wendell. "I'm not thinking of a career at all. I've just been keeping this dog at my house the last few days, and Wendell here got all curious about him because he's a dog everyone's been seeing around the last week or so, especially down by the river.

184

So Wendell here, in his curiosity, started doing some investigating work as part of his volunteer job at the paper. And he seems to think that this dog used to belong to your son Jim."

The woman paled. "Oh, no. Jim's dog . . . Jim's dog drowned, you see."

"I'm pretty sure that's not the case, ma'am," Callie said. "Even though that's what folks thought at first. But why don't you look at the dog and see?"

Callie pushed Buddy toward the door, and Mrs. Trebble took a step back, grabbing the doorknob to keep her balance. "Buddy?" she asked in a trembling voice. "Is that you, boy? It certainly looks like you, with a few years added on."

Buddy panted and whined to be let off his leash. When Callie freed him, he lay down in front of Mrs. Trebble and rolled over onto his back, exposing his belly. "Oh, Lord, that is exactly what Buddy used to do." Mrs. Trebble patted her chest with her hand, as though trying to slow down her heartbeat. "And he had brown freckles on his belly too."

185

She kneeled down and scratched Buddy's chest. "Where've you been, boy? You've surely been missed."

"I think he somehow figured his way home from wherever the river washed him to," Callie informed her. "That's the idea I'm working on, anyway."

Mrs. Trebble stood, her eyes brimming with tears. "He's looking for Jim, is what he's doing. Most loyal dog in the world. But it's been ten years. I can't believe it took him ten years to find his way home."

"I read a story once—," Wendell began, and then he paused because he wasn't sure it was the right thing to say. But Mrs. Trebble looked at him like she was interested, so he continued. "It was in my Scout magazine. About how dogs have traveled a thousand miles to find their families. One dog got lost in California, and it took him five years to get back to his home in North Carolina. But he did it."

"Isn't that something?" Mrs. Trebble said, her mouth trembling. "Well, Buddy is the sort of dog that would do that. Loyal as the day is long."

"Ma'am, you feel like you could talk to Wendell here some about Jim?" Callie asked softly. "Just for a minute?"

But Mrs. Trebble was already backing into the house. "Not today, children. I've—I've got company coming over. Why don't you come back on Monday? I'll be better prepared for you on Monday."

Wendell wondered if they showed up on Monday, whether she'd even answer the door. "You want Buddy to stay with you? I mean, now that he's back and all?"

Mrs. Trebble smiled a sad smile. "Oh, I reckon he could have found his way back a long time ago if he'd wanted to. No, I suspect Buddy's just going to keep searching that river for the rest of his days."

And sure enough, right then Buddy jumped up and turned toward the path. Giving one last glance back at Mrs. Trebble, he scampered toward the road like he was late for an appointment.

"He's a good dog," Wendell told Mrs. Trebble, and to his surprise felt his throat grow tight. He bet if he drowned in the river, King would do the same thing Buddy was doing. There wasn't nothing better than a dog, Wendell thought as he swiped his hand across his eyes. Nothing better.

"You think she's gonna open that door come Monday morning?" Callie asked as they followed Buddy down the drive.

"I'd be surprised."

Callie nodded. "Me too. I'd still like to write an article for the paper, though."

"Is that what you're going to be, a newspaper reporter?"

"Maybe. That or else a private investigator."

"Private investigator sounds like it might be fun," Wendell agreed. "You reckon that's the same thing as a detective?"

"What my daddy says is that detectives work for the police department and private investigators work for themselves. That's the main difference."

"Well, how you gonna private investigate

Jim Trebble if his mama won't talk to you?"

Callie shrugged. "Ain't sure. I was thinking I might try tracking down that Robert Lincoln, who got quoted in the article. He was one of Jim Trebble's friends."

Wendell had to admit that was a good idea. He glanced at Callie. For a girl, she was all right, he guessed. She wasn't stupid, anyway. And then he thought of something. "Lincoln's Used Cars—you reckon that's him?"

"How old this Robert Lincoln gonna be now? Around twenty-two? Twenty-three? Can you be twenty-three and own your own used-car lot?"

"Maybe," Wendell said, pondering. "Or maybe it's his dad's place. Maybe Robert Lincoln works there."

"Where is it? That place on Green Street?"

"That's the one."

Callie looked at Wendell. "You know I can't go if you don't go with me. Or at least, it'd be better if you did. I know you don't want to, though."

The confounding thing was, Wendell *did* want

189

to go. He didn't even mind the thought of going with Callie, who he decided he liked fine as a person, even if she was bossy and opinionated. He just wished she weren't colored. Or a girl. Those were the two facts about Callie Robinson that made her complicated.

"I guess I could get Carl Jr. to go with me," Callie said. "People tend to like Carl Jr. a whole lot. Even white folks like him."

"I'll go," Wendell told her, surprising them both. "I guess I'm getting interested in who this Jim Trebble person was."

"You know what I'm interested in? I'm interested in who this Jim Trebble *is*. Sometimes I feel like he's right behind me, and all I got to do is turn around."

"That's crazy. I ain't going anywhere with you if you keep talking crazy talk."

"Fine then, I'll keep it to myself for the time being. Exceptin' it ain't crazy. He could be right behind us this very second."

"Oh, it's crazy, all right," Wendell insisted. "Crazy as Halloween on Christmas morning."

Still, he couldn't help but feel a little chill

go through him right that very second. And he couldn't help but turn around.

Just like he'd thought, there was nobody there.

At least nobody he could see.

18

The Catcher Boy

When Jim saw them children heading with his dog down to the river, he just couldn't follow, so Thomas pushed him another way. When you were like them, you could get through the woods fast, no worries about tripping over vines or rubbing against the poison ivy. You just went. So they headed west till they got to this lady's yard full of tomato vines and yellow flowers. She was sitting in a chair, humming, and when Thomas and Jim went through her yard, she looked all around, like she knew something there, just didn't know what.

You ever notice that? Jim asked Thomas. How some people know you're there, and other people don't?

I ain't been around a lot of folks, Thomas told him. Mostly I stay to the cabin, waiting for my family to come back. They never come, though.

How long you been there?

I don't know. I reckon a long time, only I ain't sure. Maybe a thousand years, maybe a month.

By that time they was out on the sidewalk and could see them two children and Jim's dog walking their way. Jim hid behind a tree, but Thomas let the girl walk straight through him. It was like getting tickled by a feather. After they passed, he and Jim fell in behind them.

What do you remember—I mean, about after—? Jim asked. Did you—?

You asking me if I'm dead?

Jim nodded.

I reckon I am. Only it don't feel that way sometimes.

Jim nodded again, only this time he was

all excited, like Thomas had said something important and true.

I don't think I am, he said, his voice all a-trembling. I think I've just got to get it figured out. I mean, how to get back.

Back to life?

Yeah. You think I can?

Thomas didn't tell him no, but that's what he was thinking. Even though he didn't brush up against many folks, he'd come across some souls trapped in this world worse than him and Jim. They be thinking the same as Jim, that some sort of spell gonna get 'em alive again. All they had to do was find the right trick.

Thomas didn't go into town too much 'cause of all the noise and commotion, and there was these wagons that were all closed up and didn't have no horses pulling 'em. Spooked him. But once in a while he'd go at night, when things got quiet. Town was a full-up place, with buildings everywhere. Walking with Jim, it didn't seem like town was new to him. Maybe that's why Jim didn't know he dead. Maybe he hadn't been dead long enough to realize it.

Amazing thing was when this man who looked just like Jo-Jo Bates from back home come walking down the street and stop to talk to them children. Thomas knowed it wasn't Jo-Jo 'cause of his clothes, but still it made him jump. Whoever it was looked like he thought the boy and girl be an odd pair, but the man didn't say nothing. Just asked questions and looked interested in the answers.

Now Thomas and Jim took a turn onto a road with lots of pretty trees, and that's when Jim got all nervous. Thomas thought he must be getting close to his home, the way he strain forward like a mule pulling a plow.

Thomas kept waiting to see what that old dog would do. He be acting like he know that Thomas and Jim was right there, but at the same time he act like he didn't. Almost like the dog didn't want to know. Which was fine by Thomas. He didn't have no interest in dogs getting near him. Dogs all around the cabin that night they was running to the river, and Thomas could still hear their howling, growling voices. But the dogs couldn't get in, not with that old lady shooing 'em away and telling the catcher men to get off her property or else she'd shoot 'em dead.

Thomas wondered if the boy and the girl know they being followed. Not just by him and Jim, but by another boy too. He was on the other side of the street, staying back a little, but Thomas could tell he had an eye on them children. Mean-looking white boy. Maybe that girl a runaway. Maybe that hiding boy be a catcher man. Thomas wanted to yell to that girl to run, but he knowed she wouldn't hear him. Besides, he didn't want to worry Jim none. Jim had enough worries weighing him down.

That's my house, Jim said, pointing to a place off the road, back in the grass. He was up on his toes, almost like he might go ahead and fly there, he so excited about seeing it.

You been back before?

I've been trying, but this is the first time the fog didn't come up.

The fog?

I don't know how else to explain it. It's just when I get close to certain places, everything turns all foggy and I can't get any farther.

How about now? Can you keep going?

Jim shook his head, all sad and all.

I want to. I can see all the way up to the front door. But I'm stuck right here.

You wanna wait for them to come back? Thomas asked, and Jim nodded.

Buddy come back first, and when he reached Jim, he stopped and sniffed the air. Jim turned to Thomas.

He knows I'm here.

He know something here. I don't know if he know it's you or not.

Jim slumped a little bit, and Thomas could see he was starting to fade.

I sure wish Buddy could know me again.

Maybe he can, Thomas told him. Only it ain't the right time yet.

Jim looked at him hopefully. When do you think it'll be the right time?

When you figure out where it is you need to be. It ain't here, and I don't think it's at that cabin. Some place else be waiting for you to get there.

Without saying anything more, they started to follow the dog back down the street.

Thomas turned around one last time to see if that catcher boy still be there. Yep, there he was, standing behind a tree, waiting for them children. *Watch out, little girl*, Thomas wanted to call, but he knew it wasn't no use. Only person Thomas could help now was Jim.

19

Sooner or Later
Comes Sooner

Callie did her Monday-morning weeding fast as she could, though she was careful not to pull up anything that needed to stay rooted down. If Mama found gaps in her flower beds, Callie'd spend the rest of the week paying the price, and she had things to do, places to be. Callie Robinson had a story to write.

The minute she pulled up the last pokeweed, she was scooting down the street toward the *Advance* office, the notes she'd written down Friday before in her pocket. Oh, she had the whole story of Jim Trebble, from facts about what he liked to eat—a good slab of his mama's meat loaf was at the top of that list—to what happened on the day that he drowned. Jim Trebble hadn't even wanted to go to the river that day, Mr. Robert Lincoln had reported. He'd wanted to go squirrel hunting instead, but his friends had laughed that idea away. You hunted squirrels in October. April you went fishing in the river.

Callie thought she might write something about how a day can start out real good and then go in the complete opposite direction. That had been Mr. Robert Lincoln's theme from when she and Wendell visited him Friday morning. He kept saying what a pretty morning it had been, the prettiest morning of the spring, the sun shining after a week of rain.

"You know what my granddaddy told me the day after Jim drowned?" Mr. Lincoln said, leaning back against the trunk of a used Pontiac Chieftain. "'Son, don't never go to the river the first clear day after a long rain.' I remember thinking, 'Granddaddy, I wish you'd told me that two days ago.'"

Mr. Robert Lincoln was the nicest white man Callie had ever met. Not that she'd met too many of them. There was Mr. Creedy, the superintendant of Kenton County schools, who always had a Very Serious and Important expression pasted to his face when he came to Carter G. Woodson Elementary School at the beginning of the year to talk to the children about good citizenship. She sort of knew the mailman, Mr. Simms, who hurried through his rounds in the Bottom like their letters had a stinky smell and he was getting rid of 'em as fast as he could. That was about it for white men Callie knew by name and face.

But Mr. Robert Lincoln, he greeted Callie and Wendell like old friends the minute his daddy pulled him out of the back office. Wendell had been right—Lincoln's Used Cars was Robert Lincoln's daddy's place. Robert Lincoln was the one who did all the paperwork, as far as Callie could figure. That was probably the reason he was so happy to see them, get himself a chance to get out of that crampy little old office and out into the fresh air.

Of course his face got all sad and crumpled up when Wendell explained why they were there, but when Callie said, "Mostly we just wanted to know what Jim was like growing up and that sort of thing. What kind of boy was he?"

That question seemed to lift Mr. Lincoln's spirits. "Oh, he was the best friend you could ask for. Kind of quiet, but funny, and real nice. I mean, if Jim had two of something, he'd give you one, and if he only had one, he'd split it in half. Loved baseball and collecting things— arrowheads, rocks, snake skins. Loved that dog of his too—Buddy. I've heard a couple of folks say they've seen Buddy down by the river lately, but I wouldn't know about that."

"How come?" Wendell asked.

"I've never been back down to the river since that day."

Callie concentrated hard while Mr. Lincoln was talking so she could remember every last thing. She wanted to write it down exactly right when she got home. After her story got published, she'd take a copy to Mr. Lincoln, and she wanted him to feel like she'd done a good job representing his thoughts and feelings.

"So you said you're writing an article for the *Gazette*?" Mr. Lincoln asked Wendell when they were done, and Wendell had started to say yes when Callie stopped him.

"Actually, it's me who's writing the article," she told Mr. Lincoln. "For the *Weekly Advance*."

"That's the colored paper, right? One of the mechanics we got working for us, Lester Davis, he brings it in sometimes."

"You got a colored man working for you?" Callie asked. She hadn't seen anybody when they walked in.

Mr. Lincoln leaned forward. "Between you and me, he's the best mechanic in northern Kentucky. Everybody knows it too. But we keep him behind the scenes, in case anybody's got a problem with it."

Now, walking up Marigold toward Lexington Street, Callie thought about this. Why on earth, if you've got the best mechanic in northern Kentucky, would you try to hide it from folks just because that mechanic happens to be colored? Sometimes it amazed her how stupid people could be. You got the best mechanic in this half of Kentucky, you *advertise* it, you don't hide it. You put up a sign that says LESTER DAVIS WORKS HERE.

Soon as Callie turned right onto Lexington, she saw a crowd throbbing around the front of the *Advance* office and quickened her step. She'd never seen more than one or two people other than Mr. Renfrow in the newspaper office, and usually it was Marvin Booker and Sheldon Keyes, Mr. Renfrow's delivery boys. *There must be some big news going around*, Callie thought, and started running.

When Callie reached the office, Miss Shirley from the grocery was standing at the curb, fanning herself with a copy of Friday's paper. "Oh, Lord, girl," she said when Callie asked her what the fuss was. "Orin gone and done it now. He's calling for the mayor to integrate the town pool and stirring up all kinds of trouble that we don't need. Just look at that window. Who you think done that?"

Callie turned and saw that the *Advance*'s

plate-glass window had been shattered. "How'd it get broken? Somebody throw a rock through it?"

Miss Shirley nodded. "Mmm-hmmm. That's exactly what happened. Nobody knows who done it, though. White folks don't read the *Advance*, so how would they even know?"

Callie thought Miss Shirley had a point, though she couldn't imagine anyone in the Bottom throwing rocks at the *Advance* office's window. Folks might grumble and complain, the way Mama had been doing all weekend, saying that Mr. Renfrow was stirring up a hornet's nest, but throw rocks? Callie had a hard time believing that. No, word must have gotten out somehow. Everybody had their copy of the *Advance* by Friday at noon, which gave folks plenty of time to talk over the weekend—and to be overheard by the wrong people.

Callie hated that someone had tried to do Mr. Renfrow harm, but as a future private investigator who had just solved one mystery, she was glad to have another mystery at hand. She'd get to the bottom of whoever had thrown a rock at the *Advance* office, and that would be one more story for her to write. Plus, it would make her the hero of the Bottom.

"I best go see how Mr. Renfrow's doing," she told Miss Shirley. "I've been working some for him this summer, you know."

"I thought I'd seen you around. And did I see you Friday walking up the street with a white boy?"

"He's a friend of Carl Jr.'s," Callie said, telling the same lie she'd told Mama and Daddy on Saturday when they got the news. Man alive, news in this town spread faster than butter on a hot piece of toast. "From when the colored Scouts and the white Scouts got together to play ball during Jamboree Days."

Miss Shirley took to fanning herself again. "What was he doing in the Bottom?"

"Lost his dog. Thought he might have come down this way."

"That old yellow dog his dog?"

"You might could say so," Callie said, and then she turned to push her way through the crowd so that she wouldn't have to pile any more lies on top of the ones she'd already told.

Mr. Renfrow was sitting at his desk, typing away as if nothing unusual were going on.

"You working at a time like this?" Callie asked as she walked around behind the counter. "You practically got a riot outside."

"That's what I'm writing about," Mr. Renfrow explained. "I like to get the news reported while it's still fresh."

Callie pushed some papers off the chair across from Mr. Renfrow's desk and sat down. "It's fresh, all right. Think you know who threw the rock?"

"Some hooligan, I'd hazard," Mr. Renfrow said, still typing. "Probably a boy who overheard the household help talking about my editorial. I can't imagine anyone in our community doing such a thing."

"Me either," Callie agreed. "You think it was a boy, not a grown-up?"

"That's what I suspect. I've written other editorials that have caught the attention of white folks, and there's never been any violent response. A few phone calls maybe, a letter or two. But nothing threatening, particularly. No one in Celeste wants trouble, white or colored."

"'Cepting you," Callie pointed out. "Everybody's fussing over your editorial, even my mama."

Mr. Renfrow paused in his typing. "I hope she's not too upset."

Callie shrugged. "She's a little upset. She don't like white folks getting mad. Says it causes more trouble than you could ever imagine."

"Sometimes you have to trouble the water, Miss Callie." Mr. Renfrow resumed typing. "If a broken window is the price you pay, then so be it."

Callie pulled her notes from her back pocket. "You mind if I use the typewriter in the back room? I got my story about Jim Trebble right here, and I aim to write it in time for Friday's paper."

Mr. Renfrow waved in the direction of the door. "Be my guest. I look forward to reading— and editing—your article."

Oh, it won't need no editing, Callie thought,

heading toward the back room. Every word in her article would be important and necessary.

Taking a seat at the dusty, note-covered desk, Callie began pecking at the typewriter. "Everybody's seen that old yellow dog by now," she began. "Well, I am going to tell you the story of who that dog is."

She leaned back in her seat, thinking about what the next perfect words might be. Should she start with a description of the dog and why folks might know him, or should she start with a little bit of Jim's background? What would grab folks' attention the fastest?

The part of the story she had to be exactly right with was the part about the cabin. Mr. Robert Lincoln had said them boys would treat that cabin like a clubhouse sometimes, going up there after they'd spent a couple hours fishing at the river.

"I don't even know if that old place is still around," he'd said, and Callie and Wendell had looked at each other, deciding in one glance not to update Mr. Lincoln about the cabin. "Jim carved his name on the wall using my pocketknife. Ruined it, if you want to know the truth."

Callie had had to keep from shouting out. She *knew* it. She'd known from practically the beginning that Jim Trebble had been in the cabin. Man, oh man, was she a natural-born private investigator or what?

But she had mixed feelings about including that news in her story. Folks in the Bottom might not think too kindly of Jim if they knew he'd used the old cabin for a hangout. That old cabin was like a church to folks in the Bottom. Sure, it was a church nobody went to, and one that most folks couldn't find on a map. But it was part of their story, and nobody wanted no white boys tramping over their story.

Maybe the best thing to do was write the whole thing out and then decide which parts should stay in and which parts might best be left undiscussed. Callie nodded to herself. That's just what she'd do. She started tapping on the keyboard again: "First, you have to know a thing or two about a boy named Jim Trebble."

The front-door bell jingled, and the noise of the crowd raced into the room. "Mr. Renfrow!" a familiar voice called, sounding urgent, and Callie jumped out of her seat. What on God's green earth was Carl Jr. doing here?

"Hello, Carl Jr.," came Mr. Renfrow's calm reply, and when Callie burst into the main office, she found him still at his desk, as though Carl Jr. ran yelling into his office every day of the year.

"The woods is on fire!" Carl Jr. panted. He was leaning into the front counter like he was trying to push it over. "Somebody set fire to the cabin out there, back of the Jerichos' place."

Mr. Renfrow was up out of his seat like it, too, were on fire. "Did you see it burning?" he asked, pulling on his coat jacket and grabbing his hat.

"No, no, Wendell told me—this white boy— well, Callie knows him, is how I know him," Carl Jr. explained rapid-fire, pointing over at his sister. "Anyway, he went there a little bit ago and found it up in flames, so he ran over here to tell me and Callie."

"Did he have any idea who started it?" Mr. Renfrow asked, heading for the door, Callie right behind him.

"He said he don't know. He just come up on it burning."

Mr. Renfrow pushed through the door. "Cabin's on fire!" he called out, and his words raced through the crowd, one person repeating them to the next person, even though everyone in earshot had already heard.

Well, here all along Callie had been thinking that the cabin was some sort of secret, something folks only whispered about and half believed in, but looking around the crowd, she realized that cabin had never been a secret, not really. It had been *protected* by keeping it underground in the day-to-day talk of the Bottom. Because it was clear as day that everybody knew exactly where it was.

"Bucket brigade!" somebody shouted. "Run and fetch your buckets and head down to the river!"

Why not call the fire department? Callie wondered, but then she tried to imagine a truck getting through the woods and realized there was no way. And no place to plug in the hoses, even if a truck could get out there.

Everybody scattered at the same time, and Callie didn't know who to follow—Mr. Renfrow or Carl Jr. But then Carl Jr. made the decision for her, calling out, "Come on, Callie, let's get some buckets, and Regina, too!"

Running after Carl Jr., Callie heard the pounding of her own feet on the sidewalk, and turning left onto Marigold, she heard more feet pounding behind her. Must be Sheldon or Marvin, she thought, but when she turned to look behind her, it wasn't either of them two. In fact, it wasn't anybody Callie Robinson would ever have expected, even if you'd given her a hundred dollars to make all the guesses in the world.

No, running behind her was Wendell Crow, busting in out of nowhere, flying as fast as he could to catch up.

20

The Story Comes down the Hill

It was a sight Wendell Crow would remember all of his days. A line at least forty people long stretched from the bank of the river up through the woods to the cabin, buckets filled with water going up, empty buckets coming back down, everybody yelling, little kids crying, and Wendell right in there with them, the only white face in a sea of colored ones.

It wasn't any place he'd ever expected to be, and what he was feeling wasn't something that he expected to feel: that the cabin burning down was his fault, for trying to claim it for

214

his own. Listening to the pieces of talk coming up and down the line with the passed buckets, Wendell was putting the puzzle together. That cabin wasn't his, and it wasn't his dad's or his uncles', and it sure as heck wasn't Ray Sanders's. The only person ever to have officially laid a claim on it was named Mary Barnett, and she had used it to help runaway slaves on the way to the river.

Miss Mary. The name traveled up and down the line. *Meanest old white woman that ever lived,* somebody said, and somebody else said, *They say she started out Catholic up in Cincinnati but switched over to the Quakers 'cause them Quakers against owning slaves. Say her family kicked her out, so she crossed the river and built herself a cabin.*

They say she let it be known she a friend to the runaways, took 'em in and hid 'em in the underneath if anybody was chasin' 'em.

Wendell stood halfway down the path between the river and the cabin, his jeans soaked with the water that sloshed from the buckets as he passed them up to Carl Jr., who passed them up to Callie. He'd lived less than a half mile away from that cabin his entire life without ever knowing it was there until five days ago. Never knew about runaway slaves crossing the river at Jericho's Point.

They stopped at Miss Mary's to wait for dark and to get a bite to sustain 'em, so they have enough in their stomachs to get across and all the way into Ohio.

And now Miss Mary's cabin was burning, and it was Wendell's fault for bringing Ray Sanders up to see it. Oh, he knew it was Ray who'd done it. Who else would it be? Wendell had passed Ray on Main Street on Saturday, coming out of McKinley's Drug, and Ray had leaned in close, whispered, "I'm gonna get ya," and then called Wendell a name his mother would slap him for repeating, but it had to do with being friends with colored folks.

How long had they been passing buckets up and down the line before word started trickling down that the cabin was gone? It felt like days to Wendell, but might have only been a half an hour.

"Anything left?" someone called from down the line, and the question echoed up the hill. "Just the underneath," came the answer a few minutes later, each person passing it on to the next.

"That's where I was hiding," Callie told Carl Jr. "That's where Wendell found me."

Carl Jr. looked at Wendell, and Wendell nodded. "When I looked down into that hole, I thought it was a place to store things," he explained. "Like a root cellar or something."

"It felt strange," Callie said. "Felt like something was down in there with me. And now that hole's all that's left of the whole place."

"Cabin was falling down anyway," Carl Jr. pointed out. "Sooner or later it was just gonna be that underneath."

Maybe, Wendell thought. But maybe they would have built that old cabin back up. Not to turn it into a fishing camp or a clubhouse, but to make it, well, like some kind of museum, he guessed. He looked up the hill and squinted, trying to imagine runaway slaves coming through here, running through the woods to the river. He bet they'd been scared. He would've been.

Wendell saw the editor of the colored newspaper, Mr. Renfrow, walking down the hill. "Miss Callie," he called out. "You and your brother and Wendell go on home and change. I want to see you in my office in an hour."

Suddenly Wendell felt like everybody was looking at him, like they'd just noticed there was a white boy in their midst. Wendell kept his eyes to the ground. He'd let Callie and Carl Jr. explain what he was doing there. Except they didn't really know, did they? They didn't know the fire was his fault.

Back home, Wendell found the house empty, so he didn't have to explain to anyone why he was soaked from tip to toe, or why he had ash on his hands. He wasn't exactly sure himself where the ash had come from. He thought of the fireplace in the cabin filled up with ashes, and he thought of the name Jim written on the wall next to the door.

And then he thought of the old dog. Had anybody seen the old dog that morning? He'd thought he heard him barking when they were running up from the river with their buckets of water, but Wendell couldn't recall seeing him.

Wendell raced to change clothes, then rode his bike into town as fast as he could.

21

Some Place We Ain't Even Thought of Yet

I t had been a long time since Jim had smelled anything, but as the flames crawled up the cabin walls, he swore he could smell the smoke just the same as if he'd been standing at the edge of a bonfire before a big football game. It was acrid and sweet at the same time, burning the little hairs inside his nose.

I ain't ever stood in the middle of a fire before, Thomas said. I keep expecting it to burn me, even though I know better. You reckon we ought to get out?

Jim looked around. The flames were everywhere now, licking the ceiling, all the walls glowing red with heat. He walked over to the wall by the bed to touch it, to see if he would burn, but his fingers slipped through the flames and through the wall. He didn't feel a thing.

He sniffed the air again, but this time there was no smell of smoke, and he knew he'd been imagining it before.

We won't burn, Jim said. I don't reckon it matters if we stay or go.

A fellow had to be in a bad way if he couldn't even get burned up in a fire. That's how you knew you weren't part of nature anymore. That's how you knew you weren't like anything else in this world.

I wish I could burn down with this cabin, he said out loud. I'm tired of being this way, like I'm only half alive. I'd rather go up in smoke.

Thomas was quiet a moment before he spoke.

Don't you understand? You ain't even the least little bit alive. Not even one quarter alive. You ain't been alive for a long time.

Jim ignored him. The fire was growing louder, and the roof made ominous, threatening noises. So what if it fell on his head? Jim wouldn't feel it, wouldn't be broken by it. When the fire finally burned out, there he'd be, in the middle of nothing, just another part of the nothingness.

I'm not moving, he said.

You just want to stay stuck here till the end of time?

You've been stuck longer than me. I don't see you going anywhere.

Thomas flinched, and Jim felt bad about saying that. Sometimes he forgot that Thomas was just a little kid.

I'ma waiting for the folks to come get me, that's all, Thomas said. Ain't nobody get cross that river by themselves.

A beam cracked in half and fell at Jim's feet. Fact was, that cabin didn't have much longer before it was a pile of ash, and then what? He looked for his name on the wall, but it had already been eaten by the flames. Jim felt something hard rise in his throat. Looked like the last bit of him had finally been erased from this world.

You think you ought to do that? Harry asked, and Jim looked around for his old friend Harry Partin. He wasn't there, and neither was Robert Lincoln, but Jim could see them in his mind, standing in the middle of the cabin, clear as day, and him, too, holding Robert's pocket-knife in his hand.

"Aw, this old cabin don't belong to no one," Robert had said. "I told you my daddy said it was here when he was a boy. Claims he spent the night here once and it felt haunted."

All three boys had laughed at that. They were twelve years old and didn't believe in ghosts or the afterlife or hauntings. They might say they believed in death, but they didn't, not in any real sort of way.

Jim jabbed Robert's knife into the wall plank. It took a fair bit of effort to make the line of the *J*, the plank being made of oak and resistant to the blade. Took Jim five minutes to carve the three letters of his name, and by this time the other boys were complaining, saying,

"Come on, Jim, you can finish it some other time."

But no. Jim wanted to finish it now. When he was done, he pulled the blade from the wood and saw that he'd ruined it.

"I'll give you mine when we get back," he told Robert.

"It don't matter," Robert had said. "It wasn't any good anyway."

Robert Lincoln. Jim wondered if he'd ever come back to the cabin after that day, ever traced his finger along the marks of Jim's name.

Jim had never gone back, not until this summer. Couldn't have gone back. Twenty minutes after he'd written his name, the river had claimed him.

I used to come up here, he told Thomas now. A few times, anyway, back when I was—younger.

You still a young'un, Thomas said. Look like one to me, anyway.

The fire was roaring now, but Jim could hear a dog's howls come through the flames, high and anxious. Buddy! Buddy was out in the yard.

You don't go out, he might try to come in, Thomas said. Might try to save you.

How am I supposed to get out of here?

Through the door, just like anybody.

You coming with me? Jim asked.

Thomas didn't say anything for a minute.

You sure he a good dog? he asked finally. He a dog that won't hurt you?

He won't hurt you, Jim promised. He reached his hand toward the door and let it slip through. Put a foot forward, took one step, then another. The door was burning, but when he went through it, the wood was cold. Every part of him was like liquid, like he was being poured from one side of the door to the other.

Buddy stood at the edge of the clearing. When Jim and Thomas stepped out into the yard, he stopped howling and started barking, running toward the woods and then back again.

Wants us to follow him, I reckon, Thomas said.

Jim heard voices in the woods. Buddy barked again and headed down a path away from the approaching footsteps. Jim and Thomas followed. The path Buddy led them on headed downhill. Through the trees Jim caught glimpses of people heading uphill, heard water sloshing in buckets.

They're coming to save the cabin, he told Thomas.

Too late for that, Thomas replied. We better keep following your dog.

Wait a second, Jim said. He'd spotted Wendell and Callie in the long line of people. I want to go see someone.

Thomas followed him over to the line, and the two of them stood there for a minute, watching Wendell and Callie passing buckets up the hill. Jim wondered if he'd see Wendell again after today. Didn't know exactly where he was going, but he reckoned it wouldn't be around here. He wondered if Wendell had ever felt him nearby, or sensed that someone was trailing him through the woods or standing in the cabin while he looked around.

He always did seem like a good sort, Thomas said, and Jim nodded.

You gonna miss that cabin?

I don't know, Jim said. It wasn't home or anything. But I guess it kind of was for a little while.

Time to move on, Thomas said. Maybe home's some place we ain't even thought of yet.

And so they left, going farther and farther down, the noise of the river slapping at its edges growing louder and louder. Jim slowed his steps.

I can't go down there, he said.

Buddy barked from down the path, and Jim could feel a need in his voice, a wanting. There was some place Buddy had to be, and he couldn't get there if Jim didn't go with him.

He took a deep breath. Only, he knew it wasn't a breath, just the memory of one. He looked at Thomas.

Are you coming with me?

Where else I got to go?

Together they headed for the river.

22

The Deputy Sheriff
Pays a Call

Callie could tell that the deputy sheriff thought he was somebody special, but as far as she could tell, he was just a lanky, scrawny thing with his chest puffed out from here to kingdom come. He held a little pad of paper in his left hand, a pencil in his right, but he wasn't even bothering to write down a word Mr. Renfrow was saying. A tiny smile played around the corners of his mouth like he thought everything about this situation was funny—the broken window, the burned-down cabin, folks passing buckets of water up and down the line, all of it.

When Mr. Renfrow was done going over the facts of the matter, the deputy sheriff—whose name badge read MCALLISTER—looked over at Wendell, who was standing between Callie and Carl Jr., and said, "Now, whose boy are you? Your folks know you're spending time in the Bottom?"

Wendell, cheeks reddening, put his head down and mumbled, "No, sir," and Deputy McAllister nodded like he'd suspected as much.

"I don't reckon the news would please 'em, do you?"

More mumbling from Wendell. Callie felt like shoving her elbow hard in his ribs, make him speak up, make him say, *I got every right to be here,* or, *Is there a rule against helping out your neighbor?* He looked puny, standing there with his hands shoved in his pockets, acting like he had no idea how he'd landed in Mr. Renfrow's office. Wasn't he the same Wendell Crow who'd set off the fire alarm by running as fast as he could to tell everybody in the Bottom the cabin was burning? So why couldn't he say so?

Deputy McAllister turned back to Mr. Renfrow. "Now I hear you've been agitating for the pool to be opened to colored folks, and I reckon that's the source of your problems right there. What I'm saying is, as much as I hate to see destruction of property, seems to me you brought it on yourself. You stop writing seditious editorials, everything's going to settle down."

Callie tried to hold her tongue, but the words flew out anyway. "That ain't fair! It's a free country. Mr. Renfrow should be able to write whatever he wants without getting his window busted!"

"Let me handle this, Callie," Mr. Renfrow said, giving her a stern look. To Deputy McAllister he said, "Whether or not my editorial was inflammatory is beside the point. The law has been broken, and the perpetrator—or perpetrators—should be prosecuted."

"They ought to be put in jail!" Callie exclaimed, earning another glare from Mr. Renfrow. "Fair is fair. You think because we're colored, folks can do what they want to us?"

"What I think is that some of you down here

like to stir things up," Deputy McAllister said, his voice a little tighter than before. "In fact, it wouldn't surprise me a bit if your window was broken by somebody from this very neighborhood, hoping to get something started. Same with that cabin—which, by the way, is on Bob Jericho's property, and he ain't gonna care if it got burned down or not. He might even be glad, if it makes the point."

Mr. Renfrow pulled himself up straight as could be. "And what point might that be?"

"That nobody wants colored folks swimming at the pool. Colored boys looking at white girls in their bathing suits?" Deputy McAllister gave a fierce shake of his head. "We can't have it. It goes against nature and God."

Mr. Renfrow was opening his mouth to respond when, much to Callie's surprise, that old Wendell Crow finally spoke up.

"It was Ray Sanders who did it."

Deputy McAllister gave him a sharp look. "What's that, boy?"

"Ray Sanders. He told me he was going to do something."

"Because of the swimming pool?"

Wendell shook his head. "Because he'd seen me walking down the street with Callie. 'Cause he knew me and her were friends."

Callie's mouth practically fell open, and it looked to her like Deputy McAllister was going to faint dead away. Well, what do you know? Old Wendell Crow thought the two of them were friends. She guessed that was sort of right. They'd been through some things together, now that was the truth of it.

Deputy McAllister was staring at Wendell like the boy'd grown a second head. "You got proof?"

"That me and her are friends?"

"No, son! That this Ray Sanders was the one who burned down the cabin."

"No," Wendell admitted. "But he's the kind who would. You ought to investigate him at the very least."

At that, Deputy McAllister put his little pad back in his pocket, like he was signaling that this conversation was over. "You show me some evidence, I might. But the fact is, I can't just go after somebody because some kid tells me to. I might go talk to your daddy, though."

Wendell finally looked at the deputy. "Why? You think I'm the one who did it?"

"No, I just think he ought to know who you're spending your time with."

"He don't care," Wendell said, his voice brave and a little shaky. "Long as I ain't in any trouble, I can do whatever I want to."

Mr. Renfrow took a step between Wendell and Deputy McAllister. "Deputy, are you telling me that you won't investigate the crimes that have been committed in this community? Not the burning of the cabin, nor the breaking of my window?"

"Ain't nothing to investigate. Can't fingerprint a rock, can I?" Deputy McAllister chuckled at his own wit. "Can't interrogate a burned-up building. Sorry, boy, but you ain't got a case to make."

Callie felt flames shooting up her skin, like she was standing in the middle of that burning cabin. "Mr. Renfrow ain't your boy!"

"Callie!" Mr. Renfrow barked. "Enough!"

Deputy McAllister smiled at her. "You're still just a little girl, ain't you? You'll learn how things work soon enough."

Callie opened her mouth to say something else, but a hand clamped on her shoulder and pulled her back a few steps.

"Keep it to yourself now, Little Sis," Carl Jr. said softly. "Just let it go."

"I expect you ought to listen to him," the deputy said as he headed for the door. "He's the only one in here with a lick of sense."

Callie looked up at her brother. Carl Jr.'s face had turned into stone, not a bit of expression to it.

"Well, children," Mr. Renfrow said after the deputy left, "Deputy McAllister does not seem overly concerned with seeing justice served, now does he?"

Callie felt around her collar, surprised that steam wasn't shooting out of her clothes. "He can't do us that way," she insisted. "It ain't fair not to even investigate."

"No, it's not," Mr. Renfrow agreed. "But Deputy McAllister is not the limit of the law in this town. I'll take our case to the sheriff and to the mayor if need be."

"They ain't going to listen to you either." Carl Jr. walked over to the ficus tree dripping leaves by the front door and took a swipe at its branches. "They don't care about the Bottom, about what happens down here."

"But that's not right."

Callie, Carl Jr., and Mr. Renfrow all looked at Wendell. "The law ought to apply everywhere," Wendell continued. "What if somebody came in here and shot us all dead? Wouldn't that person get arrested?"

"It depends," Mr. Renfrow said.

"Depends on what?"

"On whether the shooter was black or white. If he was white?" Mr. Renfrow shrugged. "The law might look the other way."

"It makes me want to spit," Callie hissed. "It makes me want to spit at somebody right in the face."

"Spitting don't change nothing, Little Sis," Carl Jr. said, his voice flat. "Nothing changes nothing."

"I don't—I just don't—" Wendell stood in the middle of the room, stammering away, like he was standing in the path of a speeding train and didn't quite believe what he was seeing.

"You don't what?" Callie demanded, surprised by how hard her words were, how they'd just pounded their way out of her mouth.

But Wendell didn't answer. Instead he made for the door, the bell jingling behind him as he took off down the street. Callie shook her head as she watched him go. "Well, ain't he about worthless?" she asked, turning to look at Carl Jr. and Mr. Renfrow. "Worthless as a window fan during a cold snap, I'd say. Maybe he's the one who did it—broke your window, burned down the cabin. I wouldn't put it past him."

Mr. Renfrow walked over to Callie and, to her great astonishment, took her hand in his. "Miss Callie, I've known you all your life, and I've watched you operate. You've been an eyewitness to injustice since you first started noticing the world around you, but you've chosen to live your life as if it didn't exist. Let me ask you something. Did you know that last week your father was passed over a second time for a promotion at the mill, the job given to a white man both times?"

Callie stuck out her bottom lip. "He likes the job he has just fine. He don't need no promotion."

Mr. Renfrow smiled. "You have proven my point for me very nicely. I understand what you're doing, Callie. It hurts less not to care, doesn't it? To pretend it doesn't matter?"

Callie rolled her eyes and shrugged. How was she supposed to know? "What's this got to do with that old Wendell Crow?"

"He hasn't built up his defenses yet. Hasn't had to. So when he's an eyewitness to injustice, it still hurts him."

"I don't know what that even means," Callie said, getting tired of all this talk. Sometimes Mr. Renfrow just went on and on.

"It means Wendell Crow isn't worthless. Quite the opposite."

"I still want to spit on somebody," Callie said, pulling her hand away from Mr.

237

Renfrow's. "I want to spit on everybody in the world."

"That's not the way, Callie," Mr. Renfrow called after her as she pushed open the door and stomped down the sidewalk. Well, what did he know about the right way to do things? Seemed to her like he'd started a whole lot of trouble that didn't need to happen, just by writing a stupid editorial in his stupid newspaper. Nobody cared!

When was Mr. Renfrow going to get that? Nobody cared and nothing was ever going to change. Carl Jr. was right about that. This mean old world would just keep spinning round and round, white folks getting everything, colored folks getting nothing, and the folks in the Bottom couldn't do one little thing about it.

23

The Old Dog Goes Home

The old dog could smell the river underneath the smoke. He could smell the moldering leaves trapped by dams of rocks and sticks, the silver-scaled fish and tiny, frantic minnows. He could smell the mud and the mineral debris of stones crashing into stones as the water pounded over them.

Every few seconds he turned his head to make sure the boys were behind him—his boy and the other one, the younger one—and keeping up. The old dog couldn't see them, but he could sense them, could hear their voices making words out of air. As he got closer to the water, he could feel his boy's hesitation, and he began to bark urgently.

The boys stood at the river's edge, and then the younger boy waded into the water and called out, Come on! You ain't gonna drown! The old dog pushed at his boy with his nose, trying to herd him across, but the boy wouldn't move.

Come on, Buddy! the younger boy called, and the old dog understood. The only way his boy was going to cross was if he thought his dog was in danger. And so the old dog took a cautious step into the river, feeling the weight of the current against his legs. He might make it across, he might not. The last time the water had carried him away, he'd been young. He'd paddled hard, kept his head up, made it back to shore. This time, the water would take him for its own. But what could he do but try to make it across, try to get his boy to the other side?

He followed the younger boy over a bridge of stones, scrambling from one to the next, his paws slipping then finding a hold. His heart beat hard against his chest, beat to the point of bursting, but the dog kept going, and halfway across he felt something behind him. Was his boy following? Was he crossing the river?

The shore on the other side was gritty with pebbles and sticks. The old dog, so very tired, made his way to a stand of bushes, and when his legs gave way, he went down slowly, curling into the earth. There was a moment before his eyes closed when he remembered the old woman's porch and the food she'd bring him in the morning. *You're a good dog*, she'd say, resting her hand on his head. *You're a mighty good dog.*

24

Fair on the Face of It

Supper that night was shepherd's pie, one of his mother's favorite money-saving dishes. Wendell didn't much care for it—he didn't like his vegetables mixed up with his meat, as a rule—but he had no interest in calling attention to himself by complaining.

He'd expected a fuss as soon as he came in the front door. It was late afternoon by then, and his dad's truck was in the drive, the engine's slow clicking as it cooled a signal that he had just gotten home.

Well, this is it, Wendell had thought. Surely

word had gotten around town and over to the mill about the cabin burning down and some white boy in the bucket line. No doubt the story about the deputy sheriff who wouldn't investigate had made its way to Main Street and all the way up to Burger World. Everybody in town would know that Wendell Crow was in cahoots with the colored. Folks were probably thinking he was the next Stanley Arnette. *Why don't you move to the Bottom, you love them colored so much?* they'd say the next time they saw him.

But he'd been greeted with the usual lack of excitement when he walked into the house. His mother was in the kitchen fussing at Rosemary about how it was her job to fold the laundry and she ought to do so without being told. Missy was sitting at the kitchen table drawing a dress pattern for her favorite doll. "Wash up for supper, Wendell," his mother called as he walked past, "we're eating in twenty minutes," but that was it. Nothing in her voice made him think she had anything else to say to him.

His dad was sitting in the front room reading

the afternoon paper. Wendell steeled himself. Maybe his mother was leaving it to his dad to deal the blow. He could already imagine the scene: the paper slowly lowering, his dad peering over it with narrowed eyes, asking him, "Son, is there something you'd like to tell me about?"

The paper rattled, and Wendell's stomach hopped. What would his dad's number one objection be? He couldn't remember him saying one thing or another about the Bottom or about the folks who lived there. Would he be like that deputy sheriff, say that Wendell needed to learn his place, which wasn't in no colored newspaper office, that was for damned sure?

"I'm thinking about riding up to Covington come Saturday," his dad said from behind the sports page, and his words were so ordinary and unexpected that Wendell took a step back. "I've been needing a few things for the truck. You want to ride along?"

"S-sure," Wendell stammered. He waited, but his dad went back to the paper, so Wendell headed up the stairs to his room, wondering when the blow would fall and feeling nervous that it hadn't already.

Now he poked around at his shepherd's pie, trying to make it look like he was eating. Even if shepherd's pie had been his favorite meal of all time, he wouldn't have had an appetite for it. His stomach felt pulled tight with nerves. How'd he get himself into this mess? If he'd just stuck to his routine and not gotten tangled up with that jerk Ray Sanders, none of this would've happened. He wouldn't have felt guilty, wouldn't have felt like he had to help Callie out, wouldn't have ended up in Mr. Renfrow's office with a sheriff's deputy who was going to blab all over town about how Wendell Crow was friends with a colored girl.

Wendell grabbed a roll from the basket and tore it in two. He didn't even know why he'd said him and Callie were friends. He didn't have friends who were girls and he didn't have friends who were colored. *Nobody* did. That was the thing. There wasn't nothing wrong

245

with being colored. He liked Callie and Carl Jr. just fine, but that didn't mean they were friends. They went to different schools, lived in different neighborhoods. There wasn't anything to tie them together.

Of course, there were people like Mr. Renfrow who thought whites and colored should mix. "Read this," Mr. Renfrow had said when Wendell asked him about the broken window, handing him a torn page from the newspaper. Wendell had started to read it, but that's when Deputy McAllister had shown up. So he'd folded the piece of paper and stuck it in his pocket. He hadn't read it until he was halfway home, after he couldn't run anymore and had to stop to catch his breath.

The thing was, the editorial made sense in a way. Wendell believed in things being fair. He thought it was wrong that Deputy McAllister wasn't going to investigate who had broken Mr. Renfrow's window or burned down the cabin, especially because there was no doubt in Wendell's mind that Ray Sanders was the culprit. In fact, it made him mad that Deputy

McAllister wasn't going to do anything. Made him mad too when Mr. Renfrow said if a white man walked into the room and killed them all, he might not get prosecuted either.

"Why aren't you eating, Wendell?" his mother asked, and Wendell shoved a forkful of hamburger into his mouth to make her happy, but he hardly paid attention to what he was chewing on. He was too busy trying to grab on to the thoughts rolling around in his head. What Mr. Renfrow had written—that everybody's taxes, white and colored, had paid for the new pool, so everybody should be able to use it—well, that was fair on the face of it, he had to admit. But Wendell couldn't see it happening. Nobody would let it happen. All sorts of folks who never had a bad word to say about the colored, they'd be as against it as the others.

He looked up at his dad. His dad was a prime example of life not being fair. Why, his dad could tell you anything you wanted to know about politics or how the government worked or why a situation was this way and not that.

But he'd never be president or even mayor or city councilman. He was a mill worker and the son of a mill worker, and people like him never got to be president or mayor. That wasn't fair, but that's how it was.

He ate another bite of shepherd's pie and listened to Missy explain how her doll was going to a fancy tea party and Rin Tin Tin was going to be there, wasn't that something? Wendell was starting to get the feeling that nobody knew a thing about the fire. The fact was, if the cabin had burned down two weeks ago, before he'd met Callie, before his dad had even told him about it, he might not have known about the fire either. Maybe if he'd been down at the river and seen the smoke, but even then, what was that cabin to him? He wouldn't have known that runaway slaves had been hidden away there, or that his dad and his brothers had played there as boys, or that some kid named Jim had carved his name in the wall.

So why would anyone in Celeste care, when that cabin had probably meant less than spit to them, even if they'd known it existed? He bet

Deputy McAllister didn't even care enough to tell his boss. It was a story that didn't matter to anybody but the colored down in the Bottom, which made it a story that didn't matter at all.

Rosemary cleared the dinner plates and returned with a bowl of pudding from the refrigerator. "I made this from a mix," she said proudly. "It's a little waxy on top, but I don't think that matters, do you?"

"I'm pretty full," Wendell said, pushing his chair away from the table. The funny thing was, his stomach finally felt like it was starting to loosen up a little. The tight feeling wasn't so tight. He felt like he had things thought through pretty well. Word wasn't going to get back to his parents, life wasn't fair, he was sorry about the cabin and Mr. Renfrow's window, but there wasn't one thing in the world he could do about it.

"I'm going out with King," he said, and when his mother said she wanted him home by dark, he nodded and headed for the back door. He was always home by dark. It was hard to see a snake on the path after the sun went down.

It wasn't all that late yet, maybe closing in on seven, but the racket in the woods was gearing up. Crickets, katydids, bats, frogs, mockingbirds, and mourning doves. King's ears stood at alert, twitching left and right, and his nose sniffed the air every five seconds. Wendell liked this time of evening best, when the heat loosened its grip on the day, and cool air seemed to rise from the ground.

He took in a deep breath through his nose and could smell the smoke from the fire, though the scent was softer now, not as insistent as it had been earlier. Would the fire have traveled if people hadn't been there to put it out? It hadn't been a particularly dry summer, but maybe that didn't matter. Wendell supposed it was a good thing he'd been walking down to the river that morning, and now he felt sort of bad that he couldn't tell his dad he'd helped to put a fire out.

But he couldn't. He was already working on a story if word got out about him being in

Mr. Renfrow's office, and it wouldn't have anything to do with the cabin in the woods. Maybe he'd say he was pretty sure Ray had thrown the rock through Mr. Renfrow's window, and Wendell felt it was his duty as a good citizen to let Mr. Renfrow know. *I have a respect for private property*, he'd tell anyone who asked, *no matter who it belongs to.*

As they got closer to the river, King started to whine. Man alive, Wendell hoped Callie wasn't hanging around, playing private investigator. What was left to find out, anyway? She knew just about everything there was to know. Knew all about Ray Sanders, knew about the boy who drowned, knew about his dog—

Buddy. Wendell had heard Buddy barking in the woods that morning, so it was probably safe to say he hadn't burned up in the fire. That was canine instincts for you right there, Wendell thought. When a fire was burning, you headed for the water.

King's whine hit a higher pitch. Wendell stopped to listen for voices above the insects and birds, but the only other noise was the water singing its way over the rocks. When they reached the spot where the woods opened to the riverbank, he looked left and right as far he could see in either direction, but nobody and nothing was there.

King splashed into the water, his whines deepening now and changing into a full-throated howl.

"Where are you going, boy?" Wendell called, panicked, because he'd never seen King charge into the river that way. What if he got caught in the current? Wendell would have to go in after him, and there'd been some big afternoon storms over the weekend, so the water was full of itself, breaking hard against the rocks. He thought about Jim, imagined Jim's foot slipping on a rock, imagined his body being carried away by the water. *Only takes a second to go under,* Wendell's dad said whenever they came fishing down here. *Watch your step.*

It hardly took King any time to reach the other side of the river, and Wendell saw how he could make it over if he kept to a ragged line of rocks that spanned the water. He took off his shoes and socks and set across, feeling for the rocks with his toes, moving slow. By now King had moved ten yards up the bank, and his howling had ceased. Wendell was halfway across when he saw King lie down.

"You okay, boy?" Wendell asked King as he made his way onto the shore. He walked slowly toward his dog, making soothing noises. "You okay there, boy? Everything okay?"

King whimpered as Wendell got closer. At first he thought that King had pushed himself up against a big rock, like something was hiding under it that King just had to have, a muskrat or a toad, but now Wendell could see that King was lying next to the body of the old yellow dog. He could see that the dog was dead.

"Poor old dog," Wendell said. "Poor old Buddy." He leaned down and put his hand on the dog's head. "But you lived a good, long life, didn't you? You were a good dog. I bet you're with Jim right now, jumping and leaping, spry as can be."

He sat down next to King and gave his

scruff a good rub. "I guess it was his time, don't you?"

King put his nose on Wendell's knee. *There's nothing better in this world than a dog*, Wendell thought, and he guessed that was why he was crying, and he guessed he'd just sit there until he stopped.

25

Across the River to the Other Side

Lord, Thomas thought he wasn't ever gonna get Jim across that water. Him and Buddy doing everything to get Jim to put a foot in, Thomas yelling, *Come on! You ain't gonna drown. Water ain't got a claim on you no more.* But Jim, he didn't want to have nothing to do with that old river, you could tell.

That dog Buddy, he barking at Jim's feet, pushing into him with his nose. Thomas never seen nothing like it, especially since before today Buddy'd kept his distance. But it was like he know what Thomas knowed all along, that none of 'em was gonna be free till they got to the other side.

All sorts of surprises that day—Buddy acting like Jim a real boy again, and Thomas being the one to say, *Let's get across, let's go.* Here he'd been waiting for someone to come and fetch him to freedom, and turned out he was the fetcher. Him and that old dog. Made him laugh to think *he* the one leading folks across the river like some Moses.

In the end Thomas quit calling out Jim's name and started calling out Buddy's. Buddy come right to the middle of the river and waited, the water wild around him. Anybody looking could see he didn't have the strength to stand there too long before the water washed him away. Jim didn't have no choice then. He put one foot in the water, then the other, and you could tell he be feeling kinda sick, but he also starting to realize that the water couldn't do nothing to him anymore.

All three of 'em crossed over together, and that felt right to Thomas. That first step onto the other side? Thomas could feel it. He could feel a little bit of weight come back into him. Looking over, he could see Jim felt the same way. First thing Jim done was lean over and pick up a rock. Picked it up! Threw it into the water! Well, Thomas just had to do the same, now didn't he?

They musta throwed a hundred rocks, just 'cause they could. But they didn't dare step a foot back into the water, in case their hands turn back into air.

Jim was scooping up another rock when he seen the old dog curled up that way on the ground. Thomas knowed it right away that Buddy was dead, and Jim knowed it too. He put a hand on his dog's head and left it there a long time, like he couldn't decide whether to be sad that his dog dead or happy that he could feel how hard Buddy's skull was, how his fur was soft as velvet.

"We best get going," Thomas said. "I don't think this is where we supposed to stop, do you? I think there's something more we got to find."

Jim nodded, all sad, and stood up. He picked

off some grit from his pants and rubbed it between two fingers. Then he looked up and pointed at a tree.

"I see something, stuck in the branches," he said, and run off to grab it, just 'cause he could, Thomas reckoned.

Not even a minute later he come back with a hat on his head, and he was looking like he didn't know whether he laughing or crying.

"It's my hat," Jim said, pulling on the brim. "See that *C* on it?"

"I don't rightly know what a *C* is," Thomas said. "You mean that wishbone-looking thing?"

Jim nodded. "*C* for *Cincinnati*," he said, tracing his finger along the mark. "My name's still on the inside."

And then he laugh and laugh, like laughter this new invention he just discover.

Seem like soon as they step up into the woods, the woods change over and they in a field, a big green field with a big blue sky. Birds everywhere and flowers, and Jim gone all crazy 'cause he be making a shadow.

They spent a couple more minutes or maybe

a couple more hours throwing their shadows against the green grass until a thought started pulling at Thomas, like it might be time to take a few steps forward.

"You want to see what's over that way?" he asked Jim, and Jim said he did, said it in the same unworried way that Thomas was feeling, like nothing but good things gonna cross their path from now on. That's when the old yellow dog run up behind them barking. Thomas, he didn't even flinch! Him and Jim start laughing some more, like they know they finally where they supposed to be.

And Thomas, he knowed that was truer than true when a voice called his name and there come a woman walking across that green field under that blue sky, saying, "Hey, baby! We been waiting for you!"

And Thomas, he started running, he was calling out to his mama, "I been wanting to see you for the longest time!"

26

Trouble the Water

Callie supposed she might ought go take a look at that old pool, not that she had the least little bit of interest in swimming in it. Didn't she have a whole river to swim in? Not just any old river either, but the Ohio River, a tributary of the mighty Mississippi, running 980 miles from tip to toe. Couldn't say that about some old swimming pool, now could you?

Still, Callie thought she should take a look. She'd seen the pool before, but she'd never studied on it, couldn't picture in her mind if it had one diving board or two, or if the slide curved around or just went straight down. She guessed she ought to know.

She decided to take the long way, cross Main Street where it intersected with South Central, then walk all the way up to Elm. Maybe she'd see Buddy. She'd wanted to go down to the river, see if he was roaming the banks, but her mama had strictly forbidden Callie from getting anywhere close to the river for at least two weeks. "You let everything settle down first," her mama had said. "Might take a while for the fuss to blow over."

Mama had meant the fuss about the pool. Everybody in the Bottom was sure that's why the cabin had been set on fire and a rock thrown through Mr. Renfrow's window. Callie, she wasn't convinced. She thought Wendell was right, that Ray Sanders had been making a point about the two of them being friends. The fact was, weren't no white folks in Celeste worried about colored folks swimming in their pool, because it wasn't ever going to happen. Nobody would take the trouble to burn down some old cabin over that.

She crossed Lexington Street and looked down toward the *Advance* office. The delivery truck stood out front, and Callie thought about getting a look at this week's paper, see what Mr. Renfrow had to say about the latest happenings. But she hadn't finished her article yet, and she didn't want one of those stern looks Mr. Renfrow liked to give her. *My deadline ain't until five p.m. today*, she'd remind him, but the fact was she probably was going to miss it. The story couldn't really be finished until she took one last look at Buddy.

Callie liked a Friday morning, and this Friday morning was no exception. The middle of the week had been rainy, which folks were saying was a blessing, since sparks from a fire could pop out days later and get things going again. If the woods started burning, the Bottom would be next, they said. But the rain had moved away Thursday night, leaving everything sparkly and clean. Could almost say it was cool, Callie thought, cool meaning one thing in January and another in July.

Folks driving by in their trucks honked and

waved at her, and Mrs. Juanita Lambert said hey from her front porch and did Callie want some lemonade? Callie called out her thanks but kept on walking. Not that she was worried about losing her courage if she didn't head straight to where she was going. Why, it didn't take a lick of courage to stand outside a pool and look in. One-year-old baby could do that. If Callie had a nervous feeling in her stomach, it was probably about missing that old deadline. She might have an excuse, but Mr. Renfrow would still fuss.

Folks fussing at her—that's one thing Callie Robinson had had enough of for one lifetime. You'd think she'd gone and robbed a bank the way her mama had fussed at her when she learned what Callie had been up to with her private investigating.

"I ought to ring Orin Renfrow's neck for encouraging you," Mama had said Monday night after dinner, the two of them sitting on the porch for what Mama had billed as "a little discussion about the day's events."

"He didn't encourage me," Callie explained.

"He just helped me. It's not like he said, 'Callie, I want you to figure out the story of the old dog for me.' I came up with that idea by myself. Mr. Renfrow just let me look through some old newspapers."

"Did he know that boy was helping you too?"

For some reason Callie's mama refused to call Wendell anything other than "that boy."

"He saw us together once, but that's all. What was he supposed to do? Send Wendell home?"

Mama squinted at her. "You sassing me?"

"No, Mama! I'm just telling you the facts. Don't go blaming anything on Mr. Renfrow. It's not his fault."

"Well, his editorial about the swimming pool was his fault. That man doesn't have a lick of sense."

"You don't think we ought to be able to swim in that pool? You don't think that's fair?"

Mama fanned herself a few times before replying. "Oh, I don't think fair or unfair comes into it. Of course it's not fair. A lot of things in this world ain't fair. And I'm not saying we ought not to change them. But the change has got to be slow, or else a whole lot of people are going to get hurt."

Maybe, Callie thought now, crossing Main Street, South Central turning into North Central. She sure didn't want anybody to get hurt over no swimming pool, especially a swimming pool that might not even be worth it.

The pool was two blocks down Main Street, at the corner of Main and River, but Callie decided to keep walking north. There were some real pretty houses on Elm Street, before you got to the new elementary school, houses with wide front porches that wrapped around three sides, and little towers poking up out of the second floor. She'd like to live in one of them houses someday and have herself a maid to clean it.

Way things were, she thought, kicking a stone off the sidewalk, she'd probably be a maid cleaning houses. Didn't Carl Jr. say things weren't ever going to change? Well, her mama cleaned houses, so Callie supposed she'd be a housecleaner too.

Called stopped dead in her tracks. Now,

what kind of thinking was that? She wasn't going to be no maid! She was going be a private investigator or a newspaper reporter. Not only was she not going to be a maid, she was going to be so rich that her mama wouldn't have to clean anybody else's house ever again.

That idea satisfied her and put a little hop into her step. She'd be rich and live in a big house right here on Elm Street, and if somebody didn't like it, well, they could take it up with the president, because Callie Robinson didn't care.

Thomas Edison Elementary School stood shining at her from the end of the street, where Elm teed into Green. That's the school where her children would go, Callie thought, a bright, shiny school with a cafeteria and an auditorium and a gymnasium, each in a different wing of the building. Callie bet all the teachers who taught at Edison were sweet natured and never yelled. She'd make sure her children brought them presents at Christmas and on the last day of school, show them teachers how appreciated they were.

Well, she'd just better go look in the window if that's where her babies were going to get their education, now hadn't she? Callie crossed Green Street and walked through the grass to a window that ran the length of a classroom. Oh, it was a nice classroom too, Callie thought, pressing her nose against the glass. Portraits of the presidents from Washington to Eisenhower were hung close to the ceiling, and a long chalkboard spanned the front wall. Someone had written "Have a happy summer!" in big cursive letters across the board, with a wreath of chalk-drawn flowers and smiling suns around it. Callie bet the teacher'd had a party the last day of school, with cake and little cups of punch.

"Little girl! Little girl!"

Callie turned to see a stout white woman holding a leash. A poodle stood at her ankles, yipping in Callie's direction.

"Yes, ma'am?" Callie called out to her. "Can I help you?"

"That's not your school, little girl. Why don't you run along?"

The woman's tone wasn't the least bit mean; why, it was downright friendly. Still, Callie felt a sting and it surprised her how deep it went.

"I ain't causing any trouble, ma'am. Just looking at the nice classroom."

"But it's not your school, now is it? Why don't you run along home now?"

Callie felt like she shouldn't have to, but she didn't know what else to do. Put her hands on her hips and say, "My tax dollars paid for this school! I got a right to stand here if I want"?

But then that old white woman would probably call the police, and Callie's mama would have a fit. *Didn't I tell you to stay out of trouble?* she'd say ten million times, until the words were sewn to the inside of Callie's brain.

"I was just looking," Callie repeated, and moved away from the building. She thought about adding, "That sure is a puny dog you got there," but decided it wasn't worth the bother.

She walked a block south, then turned right on Main and walked a block west. She could hear children screaming and splashing and the lifeguard's whistle blowing even before the pool came in sight.

Her plan had been to go stand by the fence and peer in, the way she'd looked into that classroom, but now she wasn't so sure. Maybe that old lady would walk past, tell her that she needed to move along, that the swimming pool wasn't for her either. Maybe Callie would just stand on the sidewalk and look. Couldn't no one take her to task for standing on the sidewalk, now could they?

Well, she had to admit it. That pool looked delicious. Clear blue water lapping at the sides, glittering here and there as it caught pieces of the sun. Children leaped from the diving boards, one high and one low, and Callie could just imagine it, could just see herself pushing off high into the air and then doing a neat flip before she shot into the water. Oh, that high dive was just built for a girl like her.

She looked away. Something hard as hands grabbed her throat and pulled tight, and Callie couldn't tell if it was a scream building in her lungs or a flood of tears about to burst through her eyes. Now what good would that do, she scolded herself, standing on the sidewalk screaming and crying?

She looked up the road, toward McKinley's Drug, just to give her eyes a place to focus. Plenty of folks out on this fine morning, mothers pushing strollers, a boy on his bike with a dog trailing beside him on the sidewalk.

And if that boy wasn't Wendell Crow! The screams and tears in Callie's throat melted away. Didn't he see her standing there on the middle of the sidewalk? Everybody else was throwing glances her way, like what might she be doing there, but Wendell Crow didn't even notice? Callie stuck her hands on her hips and shook her head. She'd known all along he was worthless, and didn't this just go to show it?

She turned back to the pool. Standing on the other side of the chain-link fence, staring straight at her, was a little girl, maybe five, maybe six, wearing an aquamarine bathing suit and a rubber swim cap with petals on it.

"Hey!" the little girl called out to Callie. "Whatcha doing?"

"Observing," Callie told her.

"You want to come swim with me?" The girl looked down, like she'd suddenly been overcome by shyness. "You probably don't. I've got two sisters, and they don't want to swim with me either."

"Well, it's not that I don't want to swim with you," Callie said. "It's just . . . uh, I don't have my suit with me. Yours is real pretty, by the way."

"It's my cousin's," the girl informed her, holding out the skirt. "Only she got too fat. I'm pretending I'm a ballerina. That's what I'm going to be when I grow up. What are you going to be?"

Callie almost said she was going to be a private investigator, but at the last second she changed her mind. "I'm going to be a newspaper reporter. I'm going to make sure everybody in town gets the news."

The girl beamed. "That's a good thing to be! That's what I might be too!"

"Maybe we'll work for the same paper."

"We could put our desks next to each other!"

With that, the girl trotted off. Callie smiled after her. Little kids were crazy, now that was a fact.

She took a step closer to the pool, so that now she was standing in the grass. She could smell the chlorine, could feel it sting her eyes a little bit. She only knew it was chlorine because Carl Jr. had told her about it. Callie hadn't actually ever gone swimming in a pool before. She imagined how it would feel to jump in right now, not even bothering to take off her shoes. All that rain they'd been having, she bet the water would be cold as ice. Bet it'd feel pretty good, too.

"I've got something to tell you," a voice called out behind her, and Callie wheeled around. Who should be standing smack-dab in the middle of the sidewalk, his bike leaning against the light pole, but old Wendell Crow himself, his dog, King, standing by his side.

"What if I don't want to hear what you got to tell me?" Callie asked. "What if what you got to say ain't all that important to me?"

Wendell shrugged. "I reckon you'll want to know."

"Know what?"

"I found Buddy's body by the side of the river. Other side of the river, I mean. He hadn't been dead long, I wouldn't think. Half a day at most."

Callie looked at the sky. She couldn't think of what to say. She put a hand over her eyes and stood that way for a minute, just swaying back and forth. She wasn't ever getting a dog, that was for sure. Dogs hurt too much. She ever needed a pet, she'd get a fish.

"He was a pretty old dog," Wendell said. "Twelve, fourteen years, that would be my guess."

Callie shrugged, sniffing. She guessed. Might have been older than that. "You think Jim's mama knows?"

"Doubt it. I was thinking we ought to tell her sometime."

"*We?* As in you and me?"

Wendell nodded. "Yeah. I mean, she prob-ably thinks of us as a team, the way we said we were working on that article and all."

"I guess that makes sense," Callie said. "Only I can't do it today." She nodded toward the pool. "I'm doing this today."

Wendell glanced over at the fence. "I saw you standing here before, when I was riding down the street. I thought about stopping, but—I don't know. I guess I couldn't figure out what you were doing."

"Maybe I'm taking notes," Callie said, finding her voice.

"About the pool?"

"About something. Maybe it ain't none of your business."

Wendell cracked a grin. "Yeah, well, don't you think it might be handy to have a pencil and a notepad?"

Callie tapped her head. "All my notes are in here."

After a minute where neither said anything, Wendell started toward his bike, but then he turned back. "You think it's going to change anything?"

"What?"

"You standing here by the pool? You think that'll make people change their minds and start letting colored folks in?"

Callie thought about that little girl asking her to swim. Little white girl that didn't know any better. Maybe by standing there Callie had planted a seed in her head. Maybe that little girl would grow up thinking colored folks swimming at the pool was a normal, everyday thing.

"It might," Callie told Wendell. "Why don't you stand here with me? Who knows what that might change?"

"I-I don't know," Wendell stammered, his cheeks going red as cherries. "Don't see exactly what it's got to do with me."

"You live in this town?"

Wendell nodded.

"Your daddy pay taxes like mine do?"

He nodded again.

"Then it's got something to do with you."

Wendell scratched his head. "Maybe. I don't know. Anyway, I've got to go. My mom asked me to pick up a few things in town."

"Go on, then," Callie told him. "Free country."

Grabbing his bike, Wendell pushed it out to the street and hopped on, King trotting beside him. Callie watched him ride up the street.

"Don't be afraid! Jump!" a voice rang out from the other side of the fence, and Callie turned to see the little ballerina girl on the diving board, the low one, standing halfway between the stairs and the water. Callie calculated how many more days the pool would be open. Probably till school started up again first week of September. Maybe by then the girl wouldn't be afraid to jump.

Well, she'd just have to stay around and find out, wouldn't she? She could plant herself here every morning from ten to eleven, let folks get used to the idea of a colored girl at the pool. Each day she'd move a little bit closer to the fence, and then one day a couple weeks from now, why, she'd go on in and take a swim, just like that, and nobody would even blink an eye.

"It ain't gonna make a difference."

Callie didn't even bother looking up. "Why you harassing me, Wendell Crow?"

"I mean it, what's the two of us standing

here gonna change?" Wendell came up beside her and shoved his hands in his pockets, started rocking back and forth on his heels. "Why do you think life's gotta be fair in the first place? Everybody knows it ain't."

"Easy for you to say," Callie said. "You can come swim in this pool that my daddy paid for anytime you want."

"Still ain't gonna make a lick of difference."

But he didn't go anywhere, just stood there rocking, his cheeks still red, sweat beading on his forehead. Callie shook her head. Wendell Crow. Maybe he was only halfway worthless.

"You can do it!" Callie yelled all of a sudden to the little girl on the diving board. "Go on and jump now!"

The little girl plugged her nose and took a step closer to the water, and then she took another.

"Don't be afraid now!" Callie called. "Ain't nothing to be afraid of."

The little girl nodded. She took one more step and took another, and then she closed her eyes and jumped.

"Don't that water look pretty?" Callie asked Wendell, watching the circles spreading out from where the little girl had slipped in, circles stretching across the water like they might keep going forever. "Ain't it something?"

"It's something, I guess," Wendell agreed, and the two of them stood there, watching the children swim and the mothers spread on lotion and the babies crawl across the grass.

"I'm coming back tomorrow," Callie informed Wendell. "You gonna be here?"

"You mean standing next to you?"

Callied nodded.

"I don't know. I might, but I might not. I can't say."

"That's all right," Callie told him. "Because I'll be here."

"Okay," Wendell said, and then they stood there for a long time, and Callie didn't know if Wendell would come back or not, but he said he might, and that was something, wasn't it? That was the beginning of something.